Discard

D0986288

What Reviewers Say About Missouri Vaun's Work

Crossing the Wide Forever

"*Crossing the Wide Forever* is a near-heroic love story set in an epic time, told with almost lyrical prose. Words on the page will carry the reader, along with the main characters, back into history and into adventure. It's a tale that's easy to read, with enchanting main characters, despicable villains, and supportive friendships, producing a fascinating account of passion and adventure."—*Lambda Literary Review*

The Time Before Now

"It is just so good. Vaun's character work in this novel is flawless. She told a compelling story about a person so real you could just about reach out and touch her."—*The Lesbian Review*

Birthright

"*Birthright* by Missouri Vaun is one of the smoothest reads I've had my hands on in a long time. It is a romance but its subgenre is action/adventure which is perfect for me since romance tends not to hold my interest. …This story was so pure."—*The Lesbian Review*

Jane's World: The Case of the Mail Order Bride

"This is such a quirky, sweet novel with a cast of memorable characters. It has laugh out loud moments and will leave you feeling charmed."—*The Lesbian Review*

Visit us at www.boldstrokesbooks.com

By the Author

All Things Rise

The Time Before Now

The Ground Beneath

Whiskey Sunrise

Valley of Fire

Death By Cocktail Straw

One More Reason To Leave Orlando

Smothered and Covered

Privacy Glass

Birthright

Crossing The Wide Forever

Love At Cooper's Creek

Take My Hand

Writing as Paige Braddock:

Jane's World The Case of the Mail Order Bride

TAKE MY HAND

by
Missouri Vaun

2018

TAKE MY HAND

© 2018 By Missouri Vaun. All Rights Reserved.

ISBN 13: 978-1-63555-104-4

This Trade Paperback Original Is Published By
Bold Strokes Books, Inc.
P.O. Box 249
Valley Falls, NY 12185

First Edition: June 2018

THIS IS A WORK OF FICTION. NAMES, CHARACTERS, PLACES, AND INCIDENTS ARE THE PRODUCT OF THE AUTHOR'S IMAGINATION OR ARE USED FICTITIOUSLY. ANY RESEMBLANCE TO ACTUAL PERSONS, LIVING OR DEAD, BUSINESS ESTABLISHMENTS, EVENTS, OR LOCALES IS ENTIRELY COINCIDENTAL.

THIS BOOK, OR PARTS THEREOF, MAY NOT BE REPRODUCED IN ANY FORM WITHOUT PERMISSION.

CREDITS
Editor: Cindy Cresap
Production Design: Susan Ramundo
Cover Design By Paige Braddock
Cover Photo By Evelyn Braddock

Acknowledgments

This is the first installment of a trilogy set in Pine Cone, Georgia. I want to say a special thank you to my comrades in this three-part effort, D. Jackson Leigh and VK Powell. It was so much fun to work on this series with Deb and VK. It all started with a weekend in California and a suggestion from Sandy Lowe, followed by lots of brainstorming and laughter. There's heartfelt humor and genuine love in these stories, each of which focuses on one of three best friends and their search for love in a small town. Deb, VK, I loved this journey. Let's do it again sometime.

It was important to us that all three covers have a theme. My wife, Evelyn, let us use some of her photographs for each cover. Thank you!

For anyone who's curious, pineapple casserole is a real thing, and it's delicious. My friend Vanessa from Alabama has the recipe. Oh, and that skunk story is true. My grandma used to trap rabbits to keep them out of her garden. One time she was unlucky enough to catch a skunk by mistake, but that didn't stop her from insisting that my mom take her shopping.

Thanks to Susan for the assist on the segments about the motorcycle. Someday maybe I'll have a Moto Guzzi of my own.

Every published novel is a team effort. I'd like to thank Rad, Cindy, Stacia, and Ruth for all the support throughout the process of getting this story from rough concept to finished novel.

Welcome to Pine Cone, Georgia.

Dedication

For Evelyn

CHAPTER ONE

The blacktop amplified the summer heat exponentially as River Hemsworth crossed the parking lot, close to the temperature of the surface of Venus she imagined. River had just left the attorney's air-conditioned office a moment earlier, and already a light sheen of sweat glistened on her exposed arms. The humidity was probably great for her skin, but her hair was suffering.

As she headed to her car, River searched in her gigantic purse for a hair tie. Her long hair was blocking any possibility of airflow to her neck. Of course, she never had a hair tie when she needed one. She opened the car door and paused, allowing some of the heat to escape. She tossed her bag on the passenger seat, climbed in, slipped out of her heels, and plunked them on the passenger side floorboard. The blazing sunbaked leather seat plastered her dress to her back. *God, it's hot.* A solar flare was probably cooler than the interior of her aunt's 1980s era Mercedes.

Her bag had fallen open and the keys to the property, along with an unopened letter, were visible in the cave-like opening of her dark oversized purse. The key chain looked like some brass holdover from a vintage roadside motel, something from a Hitchcock movie perhaps.

River's plan was to drive over, take a quick walk-through of the gallery and the house, then meet with the Realtor. She didn't want to spend one more day in this humid, oven-baked small town than she had to. How did people live in a place like this? What had her aunt seen in Pine Cone? What had drawn her aunt to settle in here? River didn't have a clue since she didn't really know her aunt, except distantly from rare encounters at family gatherings when she was very young. There'd been some conflict between her father and her aunt that she'd never fully understood. And as a teen she'd been too self-involved to care. River had been shocked when she'd gotten the call from the attorney informing her that her aunt had left her not only her classic Mercedes sedan, but also a house with an adjoining art gallery.

The AC thankfully worked well, despite the car's age. She switched the fan to high and reached for her phone. River began to scroll through messages as she tried to heed the twenty-five-mile an hour speed limit through town. She glanced around scoping out the quaint main street, lined on both sides by brick buildings from a bygone era.

She had to admit Pine Cone, Georgia, was not without charms. Granted, Main Street was only a few blocks long, but seemed to have a thriving retail environment. She spotted a cute café and bakery on the right and made a mental note to try it for breakfast. She slowed to weave around a tow truck double-parked in front. Just past the bakery was an antique store. River would definitely take a stroll through there. She had a serious soft spot for depression era dishware. She also noted a dress shop, a toy store, a diner, and at the end of Main, a classic hardware store.

No more than a block past the hardware store, the street transitioned to residential, stately Southern homes with ancient oaks and wide porches set back off the roadway. River leaned over for a better view when a plump squirrel darted into her path. She slammed on the breaks, dropping her phone. She waited for the animal to reach the curb, then accelerated as the squirrel scampered off. She reached down and felt around on the floorboard for her phone. She teased the phone closer with her fingertips so she could pick it up. But her line of sight dropped below the dash for an instant, and her foot pushed against the gas pedal as she stretched for it. When she righted herself, the back of a horse trailer and two sleek rumps filled her vision.

Adrenaline surged through her system, her heart pounded in her ears, her chest tightened. River white-knuckled the steering wheel and yanked a hard right at the last possible second to miss the trailer. The car lurched over the curb, jarring her insides. She managed to dodge a huge pine but took out several blooming azalea bushes as the car zoomed across the lush lawn of the small white-framed structure.

River's brain processed the hand-painted sign identifying the little house as Connie's Clip 'n Curl at the same moment a darling family of sun-faded fake plastic deer bounced across the hood. The antler of the papa deer was captured by the windshield wiper and temporarily blocked her vision. Momentum and the bouncy rough ride snapped the trapped antler and the deer slid away to reveal a second obstacle—the Clip 'n Curl itself—too close to swerve and miss.

The old Mercedes must have predated air bags because the only thing that deployed upon impact was River's head against the steering wheel. The seat belt caught midway through her body's forward motion so her forehead barely made contact with the steering wheel before the force of restraint from the belt caused her body to flail back against the seat. Her hair swirled about her face like a feathery wave, mimicking the recoil motion of her upper body.

"Fuck!" She held her palm against her throbbing forehead. She could feel a lump almost immediately along her right brow.

Excited female voices cut through the pain in River's head. Women in various stages of beautification spilled out of the Clip 'n Curl. One woman was wearing something that looked like a shower cap, attached to a dangling hose. Another had some brilliant green paste smeared across her face, and two more had their hair up in giant curlers.

"Good Lord Almighty! I thought we was havin' an earthquake!" A plump full-figured woman trotted down the front steps past a sisterhood of Clip 'n Curl clients beginning to gather on the porch and rushed to the car.

CHAPTER TWO

River shoved the door open but didn't get out. "I'm so sorry, I…I couldn't stop in time." River kept one hand over her aching eyebrow and pointed a shaky finger in the direction of the truck and trailer.

"Connie, is she hurt?" The driver of the truck strode toward them.

River squinted up at the tall, handsome woman. "I just hit my head on the steering wheel. No airbags." River fumbled with the seat belt and twisted to get out of the car.

"Here, easy there. Are you all right?" The woman knelt next to the open door, blocking her exit from the vehicle.

River accepted the assistance in extricating herself, then leaned against the side of the car. "I dropped my phone and looked down for just a second to get it. When I looked up, all I saw were horses'…um…butts."

"Well, there are a few of those around here." She extended her hand again, this time as introduction. "I'm Dr. Trip Beaumont, owner of those particular horse butts. Let's get you out of the sun." Trip led River under a nearby leafy maple tree. "Connie, did you call Grace?"

The woman who'd been the first to approach the car was obviously the Connie portion of Connie's Clip 'n Curl. She was a beautiful, full-figured woman, with cascading waves of blond hair and perfect makeup.

"No, Lord no, I just ran out here without thinkin'." Connie turned to go make the call.

"Cops are on the way!" a woman wearing oversized purple curlers called out to them from the top step of the beauty salon before Connie even got to the door.

"Thank you, Lula May." Connie turned back to River. "What's your name, honey? Can I get you anything? Maybe some sweet tea?"

"I'm River...River Hemsworth, and I'm so sorry about crashing into your cute salon."

"Now don't you worry about that, sweetie, as long as no one got hurt, that's all that matters." Connie took River's hand between hers and patted it.

A woman wearing a smock covered with dancing pink piglets descended the porch steps and ran her manicured lavender nails down Trip's arm and then touched her face. "Trip, sugah, are you hurt?" River was a bit surprised by the woman's openly flirtatious physical display.

"No, Shayla, I'm fine. My horse trailer didn't actually get hit."

River's head was beginning to pound, and the blast of a siren seemed to pierce right into her brain as a black and white squad car barreled down the street and pulled into the driveway. A female officer climbed out, adjusting her utility belt and holster. She had a large clipboard under one arm. The officer was closer to River's height, maybe five foot five or six. She was shapely, not slender, with shoulder-length, wavy auburn hair. River's first thought was that she didn't look like a cop. At least not the sort of beat cop she frequently saw in her New York City neighborhood.

"Is anyone hurt?" The officer looked around the crowd and then introduced herself to River. "I'm Sergeant Grace Booker. You okay, ma'am?"

River nodded.

"Had a bit of an accident I see."

That was stating the obvious. "Yes, I'm afraid it was my fault."

"Well, I assumed the salon didn't pull out in front of you." The corner of Grace's mouth hinted at a smile.

Before River could think of a sarcastic retort, Connie jumped in. It was just as well. She probably shouldn't make sarcastic comments to cops, even one as seemingly playful as Grace.

"Shayla, run fetch Miss River a glass of something cold to drink. There's a pitcher of sweet tea in the icebox." Connie shooed Shayla in the direction of the front door of her shop.

The shock of the crash was wearing off, and River felt a little sick. She propped against the sturdy maple. The temperature in the shade was only imperceptivity cooler than it had been in the sun, so maybe a cool drink would help.

"I'll call one of my officers over to fill out an accident report while we wait for Clay." Grace stepped away from the crowd and spoke into her walkie-talkie.

"Who's Clay?" asked River.

There were already enough random concerned citizens on the scene, not including the slow-moving traffic along the road as locals rubbernecked to see what had happened. River felt on utter display, and not at her best.

"Clay Cahill drives the tow truck." Trip regarded her with an expression that either said *I'd like to take you to dinner* or *have you for dinner*. River wasn't completely sure which. She also made a mental note that Dr. Trip Beaumont had used the word *the*, as in singular. *A one-tow-truck town. Great.*

"Are you sure you don't need an ambulance, Ms. Hemsworth? That goose egg on your forehead could lead to complications." Trip regarded her with an expression of concern.

"I'm fine. Really."

Grace asked River general questions, probably to distract her from the incident, as they waited. She seemed more attentive and concerned than any police officer River had ever encountered. River tried to remain focused and answer in a neutral tone, but became utterly distracted when a large truck eased onto the grass, pulled up behind her car, and the person she assumed was Clay stepped out. As Clay approached, River realized the androgynously attractive driver was a woman. She wasn't sure who she'd expected to be behind the wheel of Pine Cone's solitary tow truck, but it certainly wasn't someone who looked like this.

Clay Cahill was tall, probably close to six feet. She was wearing faded classic Levi's that hung low on her hips, with scuffed work boots and a white T-shirt that fit snug across her broad shoulders and leanly muscled well-tanned arms, but draped more loosely over her torso. Clay had short, unkempt dark hair, and when she stood next to River, she added dreamy brown eyes to Clay's list of visual charms.

River was beginning to believe the bump to her head might have transported her to some twilight zone lesbian version of *Steel Magnolias*. Dr. Beaumont definitely gave off a gay vibe, and so did Grace, although that could just be the utility belt and sidearm tipping the scale. And now this incredibly hot tow truck driver with a brooding James Dean vibe was giving River a smoldering gaze.

Shayla returned with the tea, breaking the spell for a moment. River took a swig from the glass, wet from condensation as the cool beverage met the roasted summer air. As soon as she swallowed the sugary liquid, her throat began to close. She coughed.

There was the sort of sweet tea she'd had at the trendy southern cuisine café in Chelsea called the Whistle Stop. And then there was eating a bowl of refined white sugar with a spoon. This glass of tea was somewhere in the middle. It was so sweet she expected to pass out at any moment from diabetic shock.

"Now doesn't that taste refreshing?" crooned Connie.

"Mmm." All River could do was faux smile and nod as she pretended to take tiny sips.

"Thank you, Connie," Grace said. "You've been real helpful. I'll have my deputy come inside when she's done here and get your statement and insurance information. You can get back to your customers in the meantime." She motioned for the other bystanders to move away. "Nothing else to see here, folks."

"Connie believes in having a little tea with her sugar," Trip said, whispering as the woman being gently maligned hurried back into the shop. She set the only surviving member of the fake deer family—the buck with the broken antler—next to River and patted it on the back. "Have a seat. You look a little pale."

River eyed the plastic statue skeptically, but was careful not to poke her good eye with the remaining antler as she sat. She did feel a bit faint. Maybe it was the glucose content of the sweet tea. Her eyes were drawn again to Clay Cahill who stood silently studying her with a look that was making her heart rate twitter like the wings of a butterfly.

"Clay, this is River Hemsworth. She's having a bit of car trouble." Grace looked up from her paperwork and pointed toward the crumpled Mercedes. "River, this is Clay. She'll take care of you as soon as we finish the report." She checked her watch. "Where the heck is my officer?"

"Clay can take care of her car," Trip said, squatting in front of River and wrapping her fingers around River's wrist. "I'll be happy to escort River to her destination—just in case she has a delayed reaction to this terrible accident and needs medical attention. Your heart rate is a bit elevated."

River shook her head and withdrew her wrist from the doctor's grip and took another sip of the sugary tea. "I'm fine. Really. But I appreciate your help, Dr. Beaumont."

Clay snorted.

"Trip might have *played* doctor with a few women around town," Clay said, "But she's actually our local veterinarian."

River choked as she swallowed her mouthful of tea. She could blame it on the news that she was being examined by an animal doctor, but it was more likely Clay's whiskey-smooth drawl that sent shivers down her spine. Clay had a thoughtfully sensitive air about her as she studied River, and she wondered if Clay's sheer sex appeal caused an inordinately high number of incidents that required tow truck assistance. As she felt the heat of Clay's gaze trace the outlines of her body, she presumed that was probably the case.

River stood, looking from Trip to Clay and then back to Trip. She smiled. "Thank you for your assistance, *Trip*, but I'm fine. I should go with Clay to make the necessary arrangements to have my car repaired."

Clay didn't take her eyes off River as she pulled a bandanna from her back pocket and wiped her hands. It wasn't really that they were dirty, but she needed something to do, some task. River was watching her, and it made her nervous for some reason. She'd given River an up-and-down look when she first arrived so it was probably her fault that River was staring back.

River was beautiful. She was wearing a tailored, sleeveless dress that hugged every curve, and she had a few. It wasn't hard to imagine the yoga-fit, subtly curvaceous body under the dress. River had lively blue eyes, Clay might even describe them as bright, and long straight brown hair that just barely brushed her shoulders. She had a patrician elegance, despite the fact that she was barefoot. Clay tabled the question about shoes for later.

"Were you trying to make a quick getaway when the Clip 'n Curl cut you off?" Clay tipped her head in the direction of the car.

"Excuse me?"

"That's Eve Gardner's car." Clay recognized the vintage Mercedes.

"Eve was my aunt."

"Oh, I'm sorry, my condolences." Clay regretted making the joke.

"Eve was a fine woman." Trip cleared her throat. "I'm sorry for your loss."

"The best," Grace added.

"Thank you." It seemed obvious these three women knew her aunt better than she did. Exposed as an outsider, a twinge of uncertainty knotted in her stomach for a moment and then passed.

"Well, I need to get these horses home and out of that hot trailer. River, I look forward to meeting you again under better circumstances." Trip offered a little salute to Grace and then turned and headed toward her truck.

"Catch you later, Trip." Clay casually waved before turning her attention back to River. "Let's get your things out of the car while we wait for the accident report."

"Things?" River looked confused.

"Well, I assume at some point that dress came with shoes." River looked down. She seemed surprised to be barefoot.

"Yes, my shoes. I can't drive in heels so I took them off."
She shook her head, smiling as if she'd amused herself. "I'll
collect them and get my purse. I also have a small bag in the
trunk."

Clay followed River to the open door of the car. She stood
behind River with one hand on the doorframe and another on the
roof as River bent over to retrieve her shoes from the far side of
the car. It would have been easier to get them via the passenger
side door, but River was probably still in a bit of shock and not
thinking clearly. Clay wasn't complaining; she was enjoying
the view of the dress stretched tightly over River's shapely ass.

The car had been in the sun this whole time, and Clay felt
heat pulsing around her in waves from inside the car as she
waited. River pulled back quickly and bumped her butt against
Clay's crotch. Clay hadn't realized she was standing so close.
She could easily imagine the salacious image they must've just
presented to the crowd of onlookers from the Clip 'n Curl.

She quickly stepped back to give River room. "Sorry, I
didn't mean to crowd you."

The thought of *crowding* River was definitely appealing,
tantalizing even, but not on the lawn surrounded by debris from
a herd of maimed fake deer or an audience of overly curious
women in curlers.

Chapter Three

Clay attached the Mercedes to tow cables while one of Grace's officers spoke with River. Clay leaned against the truck cab in the shade. She studied River from a distance. Even though she'd retrieved her heels from the car, she still hadn't put them on. She stood barefoot next to Grace's official looking understudy, her shoes dangled loosely from her fingers. Clay hadn't really gotten to know Pine Cone's newest deputy, Jamie Grant, but from a distance, she was the picture of professionalism.

Clay placed River's suitcase behind the cab, leaned against the truck, and watched Officer Grant talk with River. She wondered exactly how close River had been to her aunt. Clay hadn't seen River at the funeral. In fact, most of those in attendance were locals, Eve's chosen family as opposed to blood relations. Maybe there was some backstory Eve hadn't shared. Clay had known Eve Gardner to be a generous but private person. Although as she searched her memory she did have a vague recollection that Eve had mentioned having a niece and a nephew from up north somewhere.

Clay watched Deputy Grant tuck her pen into her shirt pocket, then hand River a business card. She accepted the card with a tip of the deputy's hat, then turned toward where Clay waited. Their gazes locked with an intensity that sucked the breath from Clay's lungs. Time and motion slowed as a light breeze lifted wisps of River's rich brown hair and her dress stretched across toned thighs with each easy, long stride. She was the picture of a barefoot runway model crossing the lush lawn.

Clay shifted her stance and looked away, then walked around the cab to open the door for River. Climbing in would require a bit of maneuvering to overcome some serious elevation.

"Use the running board to get in." Clay offered her hand to River.

"I think I know how to climb into a truck. I didn't hit my head that hard."

"Sorry, no offense meant."

River made an attempt without Clay's assistance, but the step was a bit high so she dropped back to the grass, and on the second attempt, put her hand in Clay's. Clay looked at their joined hands, surprised by the warm sensation. River hesitated, meeting Clay's gaze for an instant, and then launched herself up into the truck. Clay walked around to the driver's side, clenching and unclenching her hand to dispel the tingling sensation that shot up her arm as she held River's hand in hers. That was weird. She shook it off and climbed into the seat with one powerful lunge from the running board.

"Are you staying at the B and B?" Clay put the truck in gear.

"How did you know?"

"There's really only one decent place in town to stay." Clay pulled away from the grassy lawn of the Clip 'n Curl and eased out onto the paved road.

"I'll probably stay at my aunt's place if this takes more than a couple of days, but in the meantime, I thought it'd be easier to stay at the B and B tonight."

"Well, the car will likely take more than a couple of days."

"I'm sure you're right." River was rummaging in her oversized handbag with a frown on her face. "I have a meeting with the Realtor tomorrow about selling the gallery."

"You're selling Miss Eve's gallery? What, you don't like art?" Clay glanced at River. The powerful glare River shot her from the other side of the bench seat sent warm tendrils through her gut.

"I love art." River gave up finding whatever she'd been looking for and set her purse aside. "I own a gallery in New York."

The warm tendrils crystallized into fingers of ice. Clay clenched the steering wheel and gritted her teeth to keep from blurting out some expletive under her breath. River owned an art gallery in New York. Of course she did. Look at her. Look at the way she was dressed, the air of elegant superiority hovering around her. Clay thought she'd left the cutthroat New York art world behind and now she had someone from it sitting right next to her. This was exactly why she'd come back to Pine Cone, to get away from people like River. People not to be trusted with anything as intimate or personal as your art. Clay had learned this lesson the hard way, and she wasn't going to make the same mistake twice.

"I'm sure the Realtor will be happy to help you unload the place."

River regarded Clay, whose mood had shifted so fast she'd almost given River whiplash. Such a chill crept over from Clay that she could have sworn a snowdrift had just blown through the driver's side window and piled onto the bench seat between them. She'd obviously said something that bothered Clay, but they'd hardly talked at all so she couldn't imagine what it might have been.

"Did I say something wrong?" Beating around the bush wasn't River's style.

"No."

"You just seem…upset."

"I'm not."

All evidence to the contrary.

Not more than a few minutes later, Clay eased off the road but didn't pull into the small parking area adjacent to the B and B. When she engaged the truck's parking brake, it made a loud wheezing sound.

"I'll get your bag." Clay opened the door without making eye contact.

River did her best to gracefully dismount from the high truck seat, then turned to take in the scene. The front of the quaint two-story house was adorned with a large wraparound porch. The exterior was pale yellow with forest green shutters and a neatly landscaped yard. It felt welcoming. Picturesque, that was the word River would have chosen to describe the B and B.

"I need your signature and phone number." Clay held a clipboard out to River with one hand as she placed the rolling bag on the sidewalk with the other. "I'll call when I have an estimate on repairs."

"If it's even worth repairing. I know it's an older car." She took the paperwork and wrote down her contact info and signed the form. She could have sworn they'd had a moment earlier. Some sort of connection. There'd been warmth in Clay's eyes when they'd first spoken under the old maple. And a few minutes ago when Clay helped her into the truck, well, she'd felt a spark when they touched. And now Clay was acting as if she couldn't get rid of River fast enough. She'd obviously misread the signals. Whatever. She wasn't going to be in town long enough to start something anyway. Clay took the clipboard once she was finished.

"Thank you." River tried for neutral, but she couldn't help feeling just a tiny bit disappointed to be so easily dismissed.

"You're welcome. Enjoy your stay." Clay strode back to the truck and pulled away. She'd said the words, but River was pretty sure she hadn't meant them. She lingered for a few minutes watching the tow truck shrink into the distance before she turned and walked up the steps to the broad shaded front porch.

The oak door creaked when she opened it. The foyer was basically a small open space bounded on one side by a staircase. Double doors led off in two directions from the main entryway. One door led to a sitting room with a fireplace, the other into a small dining area. A large antique desk backed up against the stairs, facing the front door. No one was around, and River considered ringing the bell, but she didn't want to act like the impatient Northerner everyone was surely assuming she was. Was that why Clay had suddenly given her the cold shoulder? Was it because she'd said she was from New York?

Footsteps on the hardwood floor caught her attention.

"Hello there! I hope you haven't been waiting long. I swear I just stepped away from the desk for a red-hot minute and here you are!" The woman extended her hand to River. "I'm Mary Jane, the manager. Everyone calls me MJ. You must be Ms. Hemsworth from New York."

"Please, call me River. I hope I'm not checking in too early. I had a bit of car trouble so I'm here sooner than expected."

MJ's grip was firm, her gaze candid and playful. "Is that how you got that lump over your eye?"

River lightly touched the swollen spot with her fingertips. "Yes, does it look bad?" She hadn't seen it in a mirror yet.

"It's not bad. I'll get you an ice pack for it, and then I bet you'll hardly notice it by morning. It's probably good that your room is all ready for you. You can put your feet up while you ice that noggin." MJ shuffled some papers on the desktop and uncovered a key attached to a brass keychain in the shape of a pinecone. "Here it is. I'll just show you to your room. It's on the second floor. I hope that's okay for you. Some people don't like stairs, but you seem to be in quite good shape so I'm sure you won't mind. Are you one of those yoga folks? You look like you do yoga."

Welcome to small town America, where everyone likes to know everything about everybody. "No, I'm not really into yoga."

"Well, you look real fit, that's all I meant. If I was twenty years younger I might just try it myself. Get myself signed up with one of those sexy male instructors who look good in tight stretchy pants. I'm sure you know what I mean."

River stifled a laugh. "I do know what you mean." Of course, River was picturing her ex-girlfriend in tight yoga pants, not some sensitive thirtysomething guy with a man bun.

River followed a few steps behind. She could see that getting a chance to speak while MJ was talking might be a challenge. MJ was probably close to seventy, but could easily pass for fifty. She was petite with a slender build and hair that had probably been dark, but was now streaked with gray. Her eyes danced as she talked. River got the distinct impression that not much got past the feisty manager of the B and B.

CHAPTER FOUR

That looks like Eve Gardner's car." Clay's grandpa watched from the open garage bay door as she offloaded the crunched Mercedes. Jed Cahill was eighty-four going on sixty, or so he thought. He rarely acted his age, especially when an attractive woman was nearby. Ever since her grandmother's passing, he'd had women of a certain mature age lining up to bring him casseroles and baked pies. He accepted every one of them with a smile and a twinkle in his eye.

"It is Miss Eve's car." The winch whined as the chain released slowly, allowing the car to roll backward. "It seems she left it to her niece who drove it right into the southeast corner of Connie's salon."

"The Clip 'n Curl?"

"That's the one."

"What's her name? Did she get hurt?"

"Her name is River, and no, she's fine."

"River? That's an odd name." He cocked his head. "She must be pretty."

"Why do you say that?"

"Someone gave her that name because it meant something to them. It just makes me think she'd be pretty to carry an unusual name like that." He paused. "Is she?"

"Is she what?"

"Pretty."

"I suppose, but I didn't really notice." Clay actually thought River might be the prettiest girl she'd ever seen. Just visualizing her made Clay's heart all fluttery. And River was an unusual name, but somehow Clay thought it fit.

"I didn't even know Eve had a niece. How the hell did she hit the Clip 'n Curl?"

"She swerved to avoid rear-ending Trip's horse trailer."

"Well, I'll be." He helped her reset the sling once the car was on the ground. "So, are you gonna ask her out?"

"Who?"

"River."

"Why would I do that?" Clay was surprised he'd even suggest it. Although, he was very open-minded for a member of his generation. Maybe it had something to do with having such a close relationship with his lesbian granddaughter.

"Because she's new in town, because she's here to settle Miss Eve's affairs." He took a breath and leaned against the truck. "And just maybe she'd welcome a friendly shoulder to lean on."

Clay shook her head. "Well, it's not gonna be mine."

"Why? I thought you said she was pretty."

"I did." She stopped fussing with the winch hooks and turned to face him. "I know you think all it takes to light a fire is a pretty face and a home-cooked meal, but I'm not like you." She considered telling him that River owned a gallery in New York, but she didn't want to rehash things right now with him. Another lecture about *not giving up* as an artist was the last thing she wanted to hear.

"Well, maybe you oughta be." He followed her as she circled the car.

"Oughta be what?" She'd been distracted by old wounds and had lost the thread of what he was saying.

"You oughta be more like me. I know you got your heart broke by that gal in New York, but there's lots of nice women here and I daresay a few of 'em wouldn't mind taking care of you a little, if you'd allow it. Women like someone to take care of."

She did *not* want to be having a conversation about dating with her grandpa.

"Can we stop talking about this?"

"All right, all right...but it wouldn't hurt you none to take an old man's advice once in a while."

"You're not old." Clay caught a glimpse of Bo in her peripheral vision. Bodean Mathis made white trash look good. He was the perfect excuse for a subject change. Clay leaned over and whispered to her grandpa. "I thought we discussed you letting him go."

"I decided to give him a second chance. Everyone needs a second chance every now and then. You of all people should know that."

Clay frowned. Her grandpa had probably given Bo eighteen chances in the three months he'd worked there. And every time her grandpa got close to cutting him loose he'd come up with some sad tall tale that tugged at her grandpa's heartstrings.

Jed Cahill was a softie for hard-luck stories, case in point, he'd given Clay a job when she'd needed it. No questions asked. But that was different. Clay was family. She looked out for her grandpa. And she worried the list of second chances he was giving Bo had more to do with Bo's grandmother than it did with Bo. The Widow Mathis was famous for her pies, and she bestowed one on Clay's grandpa at least every other week to express her gratitude for giving Bo a job.

When they were in high school, Bo's twin brother, Bradley, had climbed an eighty-foot pole and, for some unknown reason, grabbed a live power line. He'd fallen the eighty-feet to the ground and his still smoldering body had started a grass fire. Bradley died shortly after arriving at the hospital. Bo watched the whole horrible scene unfold and, according to his mama, had never been the same since. Clay wasn't so sure that Bradley's demise was the source of Bo's darker side. She'd known Bo since first grade and he'd always been a troubled, angry kid.

It wasn't simply the fact that Bo was incredibly lazy, and it took him three times as long as any normal person to do even the most mundane task. Clay flat-out didn't like him. No, more than that. She didn't trust him. Everything about Bo set off alarms for her, and the sooner she could convince her grandpa to let him go the better she'd sleep at night. She hadn't been able to prove it yet, but it wouldn't surprise her to find out he was skimming cash every time he supposedly rang up a customer. If she had any decent accounting skills, she'd likely have figured it out by now. But she didn't. She could hardly balance her own bank account, much less sort out the books at the garage. Her grandpa needed a real bookkeeper. She simply needed to convince him that he did. It was no mystery where her stubborn streak came from.

"I'm gonna get out of the sun if you don't need me."

"Nah, I've got this." Clay watched her grandpa amble toward the small office at the far end of the concrete building that housed three large retractable doors across the front.

She reset the winch. The dangling heavy hooks banged against the truck bed. When the clanging stopped, she heard a phone ringing. It wasn't hers; her ringer was off. It sounded like it was coming from the cab of the truck. She climbed up on the running board and reached for a phone with a rose gold case, facedown on the bench seat.

"Hello?"

"Oh, um, this is River." She paused. "I couldn't find my phone."

"I think you found it."

"I thought it was lost in my room, I've been feeling a bit scattered since the accident, so anyway, I dialed the number hoping to locate it. I'm sorry to bother you with this, but I really need my phone."

River did sound a tad bit fragile. Clay felt bad for giving her the brush-off earlier when she unceremoniously dropped her on the curb along with her rolling bag.

"I can bring it by for you as soon as I'm finished here. Would that work?"

"Yes, thank you so much." River sounded relieved.

"It's no problem." Clay was trying her best to sound as if she meant it, even though more personal contact with River was probably not a good idea. River was completely her type and absolutely the last sort of person she should foster any attraction for.

"Thank you." River hesitated. "I'm feeling a little out of my element, and now, without a car. I'm a bit stranded."

Clay was surprised by River's willingness to admit her vulnerability. That only made Clay more curious about this woman who'd literally crashed into her life. Curiosity would only lead to more complications.

"It's really no problem. I'll see you in a half hour or so." Clay clicked off.

Clay looked down at the screen which had a daunting list of alerts on it, voice mails and texts. River was obviously a woman in demand or very popular, or both. Clay stowed the sleek iPhone in her pocket and waved Eddie, the head mechanic, over to assist with River's crumpled car.

CHAPTER FIVE

River stared at the ceiling fan with the ice pack on her forehead and replayed the day's events. Things had not at all gone the way she expected. She'd had a preliminary call from the lawyer, but he'd insisted she fly down to settle the estate in person. Maybe that's the way these things went in small towns; maybe this couldn't have been handled remotely. But her schedule in New York was hectic. Summer was a busy time for the gallery, with all the tourist traffic in the city, and the last thing she had time for was languishing for days in Georgia.

She'd hoped to move up the meeting with the Realtor to this afternoon, but that wasn't going to happen now. It was late and she was without transportation and without her phone. She considered calling from a landline and asking the Realtor to pick her up, but after all the excitement she just wasn't feeling up to it.

After MJ delivered the ice pack as promised, River had been content to lie on the bed for a half hour and stare at the ceiling while she waited for Clay to arrive. The last thing she wanted was to bother Clay, who was so clearly ready to be rid of her, but since Clay had her phone there seemed to be no other option except to see each other again.

River adjusted the ice pack and exhaled slowly, willing herself to relax. She almost never had down time like this. It felt a bit surreal, like some out-of-body experience. She rotated her head slowly to take in the room. The décor was an explosion of country chic. The quilt on the bed looked hand-stitched, a watercolor painting of a red barn in a grassy field was centered over the headboard of the heavy oak bed frame, and the wallpaper she could see through the bathroom door was a throwback to something she'd seen from the 1950s. A faint blue repeat pattern of a boy and girl carrying milk jugs, interspersed with a split rail fence.

A vase of fresh cut flowers rested on the dresser, the mirror just behind multiplying the colorful display by two.

This was a nice room. It reminded River of her grandparents' old farmhouse in upstate New York. She closed her eyes and let her memories roam about in the fresh cut grass of their huge front yard. The weathered barn was a stone's throw from the house, and in July, an oversized American flag had waved from the flagpole mounted high on the front of the barn in honor of the Fourth. Being there as a teen was like walking onto the set of *Footloose*. Pickup trucks, barn dances, and sneaking sips of whiskey at tailgate parties.

She was such a different person now. Or was she?

River loved New York City. The energy, the challenge, the art community, there was no other city like it in the world. And the city never slept. If she felt like dinner at two a.m., she could easily find it, along with a willing companion. River had lots of friends, some with benefits. She'd gone on a few casual dates since she and Diane had broken up six months earlier. Theirs had been a friendly parting, a divergence of chosen paths. They'd been drifting for a few months prior to the breakup, almost more roommates than lovers, and in the end, had parted as friends. Diane had taken a job in LA, which made it easier for both of them to move on.

River had no intention of leaving New York. She'd grown up in a small town, but once she'd left for college in the city she'd never looked back, never even considered moving back home after graduation. What would an art history major, a gallery owner, do in a town whose idea of fine art was barn paintings and lighthouses? The thought of it made her cringe.

Plus, her father had never been comfortable with the fact that she was a lesbian. If she'd gone home she'd have felt pressure to hide who she truly was. Having experienced the freedom of the city, she knew she could never go back to a life lived with one foot in the closet simply to make things easy for her parents. She wasn't going to rub their noses in it, but she wasn't going to hide her sexuality either. New York was a place that allowed her to thrive, so she'd stayed.

A delicious smell wafted up from downstairs. Was that fresh bread? River's stomach reminded her she'd missed lunch. Maybe MJ had something in the kitchen to remedy that. She slipped off the bed and trotted downstairs barefoot.

"Something smells delicious."

"My potato bread." MJ held a bread pan between two large floral print oven mitts, smiling broadly. "I try to make it at least once a week. There's nothing better when it's right out of the oven. Shall I cut you a slice?"

River nodded. She waited expectantly as MJ slathered a healthy portion of butter on the hot bread and then handed it to River.

Boot steps on the hardwood floor caused her to turn just as she'd taken a huge bite. Clay was looking at her with an expression she couldn't quite read. Was she amused or appalled?

"I see you've discovered MJ's famous potato bread." Clay took a step in her direction.

"Mmm, mmm," was the best River could manage until she swallowed. She couldn't believe Clay showed up just in the moment she had her mouth stuffed and was barefoot again, not to mention the light purple lump on her forehead. *Yeah, River Hemsworth, you're really something.*

"Here's your phone." Clay held the device out to her.

"Thank you." River got a faint rush as her fingertips brushed against Clay's palm. "I'm so sorry you had to make a special trip over here just for this."

MJ was scuttling around in the background, slicing the warm bread, and stacking serving plates.

"Clay, sit a spell and have a slice of this while it's hot." MJ motioned to one of the nearby tables.

"Um, I should probably get going." Clay seemed anxious to leave, and River couldn't help feeling a bit slighted by Clay's obvious desire to escape.

"You sit down, I insist." MJ came over with a plate and handed it to Clay. She was clearly not taking no for an answer. "You're so lanky a strong wind could blow you over. Sit down and eat something."

"Yes, ma'am." Clay dropped into a nearby chair.

Clay seemed to relax a bit. Like when they'd first met under the maple tree outside the Clip 'n Curl. River thought of taking the seat opposite Clay, but then hesitated, second-guessing her ability to read Clay's mood.

"You can join me if you like." Clay must have sensed her uncertainty.

"If you don't mind." River took another offered slice from MJ on a small plate and carried it over to the table with Clay.

"Now, you girls keep an eye on things out here while I go see about the second loaf." MJ had a look of mischief, and

River wondered if there was a second loaf or if MJ was simply conspiring to leave them alone together.

This was sort of a perfect second meeting. As if they were in some quaint café on a first date. River reminded herself of the cold shoulder Clay had given her earlier and tempered her enthusiasm about having a real date with James Dean's lesbian twin sister.

"Thank you again for bringing my phone so quickly."

"No problem."

"Are you, um, off duty for the day? I don't actually know how the whole tow truck thing works." River was trying to find out what Clay's schedule was without sounding condescending or overly nosy.

"Well, with a tow truck you're kind of on call all the time. It's not like accidents only happen between nine and five." Clay finished off her slice of bread and leaned casually back in her chair. "We get calls from the sheriff's department about impounds and wrecks. AAA also puts in calls, and then we get direct calls from locals."

"You said we." River remembered Grace saying there was only one tow truck in Pine Cone.

"By we, I mean the Cahill Garage that my grandpa owns. I'm pretty much the only one that drives the sling these days."

"The sling?"

"It's what we call a truck with an old school wheel lift."

"Oh." This conversation was like trying to communicate with someone for whom English was not a first language. Or maybe River was the one speaking the foreign tongue.

They were quiet for a moment or two, awkwardly so. It seemed River had forgotten how to manage small talk when Clay was around, and Clay wasn't helping to fill the silence.

"Well, I suppose I should be going before MJ tries to feed me dinner too."

River stood as Clay got up from her chair.

"Thank you again." River held up her phone and wiggled it in the air.

"You were probably just a little rattled after the wreck, and that's how you ended up losing your phone."

"Probably." River had the urge to follow Clay to the door, but decided against it. She simply waved as Clay left and then sank to her chair with her chin in her hand. Clay was a hard one to figure. She didn't strike River as someone whose sole purpose in life was driving a tow truck in a small Georgia town. Not that there was anything wrong with that. She had to admit that the whole sexy mechanic thing was intriguing, but there must be more to the story than she was getting.

CHAPTER SIX

Clay parked her vintage Ford pickup behind Trip's large double axle truck, both parallel to the two-lane dirt road in a wide, gravel pullout. Clay chuckled at how her ride was dwarfed by Trip's. Grace's road-weary Corolla was parked on the other side of the road. This was the spot on the Altamaha River where Clay, Trip, and Grace had been meeting ever since high school to solve all the world's problems. It was their secret spot. Discernible by nothing more than a faded mile marker along an unpaved county road, but it was one of Clay's favorite places in the whole world. A six-pack of beer and the lazy waters of the Altamaha could sooth many hurts. They called their spot Mosquito Alley. Aptly named for the pesky occupants.

The water's source was somewhere in the mountains of the Cherokee Nation, and by the time it reached the pine-forested plain of southeastern Georgia, it had become a wide river, gently winding its way through a vast green for nearly a hundred miles, until it emptied into the Atlantic. A variety of trees and bushes crowded the river's edge: wax myrtle, sweet bay magnolia, spicebush, and red bay.

In Clay's opinion, there was no sweeter scent than a magnolia flower. The memories associated with that floral scent were stitched as delicately as a handmade quilt all the way back to her childhood.

She hefted the small cooler off the seat beside her and walked the narrow trail through the thick green shrubbery. Some might consider this a boat launch, but only for a canoe. There wasn't enough room in the dirt pullout for a trailer of any kind. She could hear the soft murmur of voices as she broke through the wall of green onto the sandbar where Trip and Grace were already lounging. Trip had a beer, Grace held a glass of white wine, and a small cooler sat between them on a slim finger of sand where the water had eaten away at the grassy riverbank. Trip and Grace sat on the grass. Grace dug her toes in the damp sand at the water's edge.

"Hey, Paintball. It's about time you got here." Trip reclined on one elbow and took a swig of her beer.

Paintball was the CB handle she'd had since high school, when cell service was even spottier than it was now in rural South Georgia. The nickname was a reminder of an awkward teenage failure, the sort of nickname that only your closest friends could bestow.

It was all Suzan Cooper's fault. Sure, she spelled Susan with a z, but that wasn't Suzan's greatest charm. In fact, she had a few. Suzan was one of the first girls in junior high to need a bra and shamelessly flaunted that fact. She was a complete flirt, and Clay quickly and completely fell under Suzan's spell.

Suzan's family was one of the wealthiest in Pine Cone, and for her fourteenth birthday her parents threw a lavish party that included a paintball competition. Clay was on the opposing team and Suzan, knowing that Clay carried a horrible crush, used it to her advantage. She played the victim, and the minute Clay put down her weapon, Suzan pelted her with bright red paintballs. Trip never let her live it down, and the nickname stuck.

Trip's handle was Fast Break, from her prowess on the basketball court. And Grace's call sign was Glitter Girl due to a lip gloss phase she'd since outgrown.

"It's that damn Bo Mathis. He kept skulking around the garage, and I couldn't lock up until he left." Clay took a bottle from her cooler, popped the cap, and then used the red-topped cooler for a seat. She strategically didn't mention the side trip to drop off River's phone.

"I thought your granddad let him go after he almost set the place on fire?" Grace pulled her hair back and tamed it with a hair tie. She'd obviously taken time to stop by her place first to change out of her uniform into shorts and a T-shirt.

The air was warm and thick with humidity, and Clay was feeling overdressed in jeans and boots. She decided to take the boots off so that she could sink her feet into the cool, damp sand at the water's edge. The riverbank was barely higher than the water level and mostly covered in dense green shrubbery and pine trees, except for the occasional sandbar that climbed out of the water to sun itself along the shoreline.

"I talked to my grandpa again today about cutting Bo loose, but he's decided to give him a second chance."

"Wouldn't this be more like his twelfth chance?" Trip snorted.

"Yeah, maybe. I sort of lost track." Clay took a long swig of her beer.

"Well, in other news, I heard from MJ that you dropped River off earlier today at the B and B. How'd that go?" Grace refilled her wine glass from a bottle in the cooler.

"I dropped her off, along with her luggage and took her car to the shop."

"And?" Grace tweaked an eyebrow.

"And nothing."

"Okay, hold on a minute." Trip came to life. She leaned forward with her elbows on her knees and regarded Clay with a serious scowl. "You had the hottest woman to land in Pine Cone in the past five years in your truck and you just…dropped her off? No offer to show her around? No invitation for dinner out?"

"No, I—"

"Hottest woman in the last five years? Who'd I miss?" Grace cut Clay off.

"Remember the grad student that was working in Judge Freemont's office? What was her name…"

"Oh, yeah. She *was* pretty." Grace nodded in agreement and air toasted Trip with her glass. "Her name was Shannon. She was too young for you, by the way."

"Hey! That was five years ago. I was a lot younger then." Trip shuffled sand in Grace's direction with her foot.

"Sorry for the interruption, Clay. Please continue." Grace relaxed back onto her elbows again and sipped her wine.

"There's nothing else to tell. I dropped her off, end of story. Oh, and then she forgot her phone in my truck, and I took that over to her on my way here." Trip and Grace stared at her for an awkwardly long silent minute. "Why are you giving me that look?"

"What look?" Trip furrowed her brow. "This look? The one that says you're a *dumb ass*?"

"I can't deal with getting involved with anyone right now." Clay's last romantic involvement with a woman had gone down in a fireball. She'd barely survived with any dignity intact.

"That's right, you don't need any *serious* involvement. That's why River is the perfect girl for you. She's not local. She's only here for a few days…a week tops…*and* she's clearly into you."

"Into me?" Clay wasn't so sure, and it didn't matter if she was.

"Yes, which is why I wouldn't let Trip hit on her." Grace playfully shoved Trip's shoulder. "And trust me when I say she wanted to, with that whole *doctor* routine after River wrecked her aunt's car…Puleez."

"Hey, I'm only human. I have a weakness for damsels in distress, especially the pretty ones." Trip grinned and took a long pull of her beer.

"Anyway, as we were saying, River was definitely checking you out. In an *I'd like to go on a date with you* kind of way." Trip nodded in support of Grace's assessment.

"I just can't do it." That familiar knot rose in Clay's chest, a tightness where her heart should be. "And if you'd ever gotten your heart stomped on like I did you'd understand." She looked at Trip. "You're always the one doing the leaving, so you don't ever have to find out what it feels like to be the one getting left."

"Ouch." Trip mimicked being skewered in the chest, her fingers curled around an invisible knife. "Listen, I've had my disappointments, same as Grace, same as you, but I don't wallow in them the way you're doing." Trip sounded like a cross between a stern parent and motivational softball coach. "You need to get out and start dating again."

"You act like it's been years since Veronica and I split up. It's only been a few months. I deserve to wallow a little."

A knowing look passed between Trip and Grace.

"Oh no, don't go trying to set me up. I can read your minds you know." They were her closest friends and she knew they only had her best interests at heart, but dammit, she wasn't ready to date.

Casual sex wasn't going to work for her. And she certainly wasn't ready to date someone like River, not when her self-esteem was at a lower elevation than Death Valley and her spirit just as desolate. She was in a low place all around and had no business inflicting that on anyone else.

❖

It was dark by the time Clay reached the warehouse space she rented on the far end of town. The large, open space had previously been a packing house for peaches, and on especially warm days you could still smell the sweet hint of fruit.

When she'd returned to Pine Cone, she'd needed room to breathe.

She couldn't bring herself to move back into her grandparents' tiny frame house, and she didn't want to be trapped in some boxy apartment. She'd been lucky to stumble across the For Rent sign for this place a day after she returned home.

The warehouse was barely functional for housing, with exposed, weathered brick that bore scuffs of various shades of previous paint colors, and rugged exposed beams across the vaulted ceiling. Rudimentary plumbing ran down the walls at opposite sides of the large main living space. On one side, there was an industrial sized sink mounted to the wall, on the other, a bathroom set apart from the room with partial walls made of glass blocks. There was no tub, only a shower, a toilet, and a vintage pedestal sink.

If she felt like painting, this would be the perfect studio. Plenty of fresh air from large crank style windows all across the upper part of the front and back wall. And concrete floors that could withstand any number of spilled or spattered disasters. There was even a drain in the floor in the event that the entire place needed to be hosed down.

But she wasn't painting. She hadn't painted anything since leaving New York. Naked canvases were stacked along the wall, surrounding her, holding her captive. Frequently, when sleep eluded her, she'd pour herself a whiskey and pace in front of the vacant canvases waiting for inspiration to find her. Nothing came of it.

Canisters of liquid acrylic paint lined metal shelves along the back wall. Colors dripped down the sides, tempting her to open them, but still she didn't. She'd considered loading up all the art supplies and unused canvases and hauling them out behind the warehouse and lighting a bonfire. She'd sacrifice the virgin canvases to the art gods in hopes of finding some peace. But she hadn't done that either, yet.

There were a few finished paintings on the other side of the large open room. Equally spaced along the floor, leaning against the wall. These five paintings were almost the most painful things in the room, so of course she kept them where she could see them at all times, to remind her not to be stupid, to remind her not to forget. These were the five paintings that hadn't sold in her solo show in New York. The show that had been the bright beginning of the catastrophic end, all in the same twenty-four hours.

An industrial looking wrought iron floor lamp stood near the paintings. After Clay pulled one more beer from the refrigerator, she switched on the light and stood looking at what had been her future, on five vibrantly colored canvases.

The gallery had been packed. Buyers had already claimed most of the pieces. Clay's head had been spinning from all of the attention. It had almost been too much.

Veronica wanted Clay to go out for a celebratory late dinner with some of her more ardent patrons, but Clay was spent. Being mostly an introvert, she'd already far exceeded her capacity to mingle and make small talk. She'd thanked Veronica and begged off. She was high on life and art and wanted some time alone to allow all of it to sink in.

The next morning, Clay had picked up coffee and scones and headed to Veronica's place to surprise her. It turned out Clay was the one who got the surprise when she discovered Veronica in bed with another woman. To add insult to injury, a woman who'd bought two of Clay's paintings the previous night at the opening.

Veronica didn't even try to explain the woman in her bed. And Clay stood at the bedroom door holding breakfast for Veronica like an idiot. Like someone who couldn't quite wrap their head around what they were seeing. She was hurt and embarrassed to have been so easily played. Clearly, Veronica hadn't taken her seriously.

What do you say when you find your lover in bed with someone else?

Clay'd been replaying the scene in her head and crafting clever monologues she wished she'd delivered. But she'd said nothing. She'd just stood there, holding blueberry scones, exposed as the novice she was. She'd been out of her depth with Veronica.

That was part of the problem of being with Veronica. She always made Clay feel just the least bit unsafe, at risk, unsettled. Being with Veronica was like perpetually flailing in the deep end of the pool. It wasn't a good feeling, and in truth, Clay had begun to grow tired of Veronica's little head games, but she hadn't said as much to Veronica.

On some level, she'd hoped that Veronica sensed Clay needed her after the show. That what Clay wanted was some assurance that Veronica was with her because of who she was, not because of the success of her work. But it turned out she was simply Veronica's pet project of the moment and she'd obviously moved on without giving Clay the courtesy of a heads-up.

Clay dragged a chair over in front of the canvas on the far right and sat down. This was the last one she'd painted, and she couldn't separate what had happened with Veronica from the rendering in front of her. She hated this one most of all. Everything she'd felt at her highest point, right before the exhibit opened, was smeared across the canvas. It mocked her.

It wasn't that she'd really thought what she and Veronica had was true love. Thinking back, she knew it wasn't. But she'd thought they at least had respect for one another, enough respect to be honest. As it turned out, Clay was the only one being honest, and once the show was over and a success, Veronica was finished with her. She'd been discarded and now she was completely off center and uninspired. Nothing came to her. Color, the strongest part of her artistic voice, held no meaning for her.

She reached for the canvas, carried it over, and dropped it onto the floor in the center of the room. The paint canisters stared back at her until she reached for the only color that made sense, black. Holding the jar about three feet above the prone, already painted surface, she drizzled black acrylic with slow, circular motions. After using nearly the entire jar, hues of red and violet still peeked through the dark wet ooze. She knelt beside the canvas and used the palm of her hand to smear the viscous liquid in sweeping arcs.

Clay stood, pulled a cloth from her back pocket, and methodically wiped the paint from her hand. The entire canvas was black now, just like her mood, perfect.

Clay finished the beer and then heaved the empty beer bottle across the room in a half-hearted attempt to hit the large plastic trash bin. She missed. The loud clatter of glass shattering on concrete was oddly satisfying.

She crossed the room to tumble facedown onto a king-sized mattress on the floor. The broken glass and the defaced painting, along with her wounded heart, would still be there in the morning.

CHAPTER SEVEN

At seven thirty the next morning, the scent of warm cinnamon rolls was wafting upstairs. By eight thirty, the temptation was more than River could tolerate. She trotted downstairs to the dining room.

She was surprised to see the police officer that'd been at the accident scene the day before sitting at a small window table covered with a red gingham tablecloth sipping coffee. What was her name? Oh yes, Grace Booker.

River returned Grace's smile as she served herself coffee from a large carafe and eyed the tray of pastries.

"You should try one. MJ's cinnamon rolls are not to be missed." Grace smiled over the rim of her coffee cup.

"If they taste half as good as they smell, then I'm in serious trouble." River used a silver spatula to hoist one of the generously sized buns, oozing icing on all sides onto a small china plate.

She turned, breakfast in hand, considering where she should sit.

"Please join me." Grace motioned toward the empty chair across from her. "That is unless you're less of a morning person than I am and would prefer some alone time."

"Not at all. Thank you for the invitation." Sitting across from Grace in uniform was a little bit intimidating before coffee, but River did her best to relax.

Grace's auburn hair tumbled around her shoulders softening the law-and-order aspect of her attire. Grace's green eyes reflected the early morning sunlight from a nearby window and practically sparkled. She smiled at River, and River decided right then, in another life, she and Grace would have been friends. If she weren't living in New York and Grace wasn't living in Georgia.

River had never really known anyone who was a police officer before. There'd been a sheriff in the small community where she grew up, but he'd been a friend of the family and a lot less intimidating. River tasted the coffee. It was better than she expected, rich and full of flavor. She was glad she hadn't been overcautious by adding sugar. She certainly wasn't going to need sugar if she ate the cinnamon roll in front of her.

"How is your head this morning?"

"Excuse me?"

"Where you bumped your head on the steering wheel."

"Oh." River ran her fingers over the raised spot above her eye. She'd tried to cover the faint purple of the injury with powder. "It doesn't hurt. MJ was kind enough to give me an ice pack for it yesterday. That really helped."

"Good." Grace studied her. "It doesn't even show."

River smiled and forked a small bite of the pastry into her mouth and couldn't stop the involuntary moan of contentment. "Hmm, so yummy."

"Hmm, yes. Yummy indeed." Grace's words were barely audible.

River followed the trajectory of Grace's gaze and knew right away that Grace wasn't talking about MJ's cinnamon rolls.

A woman was standing near the serving table pouring coffee into a paper cup. Short ebony hair contrasted with pale complexion on a tall androgynous body dressed in jeans and a plaid shirt. She glanced in their direction briefly, almost shyly, and then left.

"I was talking about the pastry, not tall, dark, and gorgeous over by the coffee pot."

Grace laughed. "You saw that, huh?"

"Was that your attempt at subtlety?" River smiled around another bite of the heavenly pastry.

"Maybe I need more practice." Grace sighed.

"Do you know her?"

"I wouldn't say I *know* her." Grace leaned forward, holding her coffee cup with both hands, spinning it on its saucer. "But I'd like to. That's Dani Wingate. She's the new veterinarian at Trip's clinic."

"Well, she's super cute." River was reminded of another tall, dark, androgynously good-looking woman. But did she dare ask Grace about Clay? She took another bite, closed her eyes, and savored the sweetness.

"This is the best cinnamon roll I've ever had."

"I warned you." Grace laughed.

"Does MJ make these every morning?" River blinked rapidly as the glorious cocktail of caffeine and sugar started to kick in.

"Thankfully, no. If she did, I'd be as big around as this table."

"Do you…do you live at the B and B?" River didn't want to pry, but the question popped out before she could stop it. She blamed the sugar rush.

"No, I own it. I live in the cottage out back." Grace motioned with her thumb over her shoulder. "I inherited this place from my parents."

"Wow, you're a police officer and you run a B and B? When do you sleep?"

"I probably wouldn't if it weren't for MJ. She keeps everything running smoothly for me. And in return, I get to eat breakfast here every morning."

"Well, it's a beautiful place. Very charming and inviting."

"I hope you don't feel pressured to say that because I'm armed."

River laughed. "Not at all."

"Good."

"Wait, that means Dani is staying here? At your B and B?" River's brain was finally waking up. Her ability to add one plus one improving by the minute.

"Yes."

"So, you get to see Dani coming and going every day?"

"Yes, it's torture. Thanks for noticing."

"I'm so sorry."

They both laughed.

River relished a few more bites of the warm cinnamon roll between sips of coffee.

"I don't suppose you know where I could get a rental car?"

"There isn't a place anywhere close. I'd say the nearest rental office would be over in Savannah."

"Oh." Wow, this really was a small town.

"But I think they might have a loaner you could use at Cahill's shop, where Clay took your car."

"Really?" River took note of the tiniest tightening in her stomach at the mention of Clay's name. The thought of seeing Clay again was definitely appealing. "I was supposed to meet the Realtor today to go over my aunt's property. I suppose I could call her and see if she'd come pick me up—"

"No, I don't think that'll be necessary. I'm sure Clay can get you a loaner." Grace finished her coffee. "I was about to drive to work. I could drop you off on my way if you like."

"If it's no trouble."

"None at all." Grace stood. One side of her mouth tipped up playfully. "Then you'll have a chance to see Clay again."

"I suppose I need some lessons in subtlety too." River followed Grace toward the door.

"Heightened observational skills are part of my job." Grace turned partway to look at River.

"Noted." River wondered how close Grace was to Clay. It was conceivable that they'd even dated. She decided to be brave and ask. "So, you know Clay well?"

"Clay and I have been close since high school. She and Trip are my closest friends."

Friends. River relaxed. If they'd been involved at some point they weren't any longer. River was dying to ask more about Clay, but tempered her curiosity. Clay had been anxious to get rid of her yesterday; maybe the attraction was completely one-sided. River wouldn't know for sure until she saw Clay again.

Clay was aimlessly paging through Eddie's most recent issue of *Hotrod* magazine, when someone cast a shadow from the door over the desk where she was seated. She looked up to see River, backlit by the bright morning sun, hands on her hips, looking like perfection itself. It didn't matter how beautiful she was in her pencil skirt, form-fitting sleeveless silk blouse, and tasteful heels, Clay refused to stop thumbing through the magazine to look at her.

River cleared her throat and stepped closer to the desk.

"Yes, can I help you?" Clay nonchalantly leaned back in her chair as if she'd only just noticed her. So that River would get that message loud and clear that Clay was not impressed. Not interested. She willed her libido to fall in line.

"Do you have any details about when my aunt's car will be repaired?"

Clay glanced through the small door that connected the front office with the shop door. Eddie stood up from the open hood he'd been leaning under and shrugged in answer to her silent question. She turned back to River.

River's arms were crossed, her expression neutral, but energy pulsed off her. As if she was daring Clay to give her the runaround. Typical New Yorker attitude.

"A few days at least. The insurance adjuster hasn't even been by to look at it yet."

"Do you possibly have a loaner I could use while I wait for repairs?"

"How'd you get here anyway?" Clay craned her neck to examine the parking spaces in front of the office. All were empty.

"The officer from yesterday, Grace Booker, dropped me off on her way to the station."

Clay frowned. Grace had set her up.

"Well?"

"Well what?"

"Do you have a rental available?"

"No."

"Can you please make an attempt to communicate in more than one syllable at a time?"

"Yes." Clay tried to look serious, but she couldn't stop the grin.

River seemed to relax a little. She shifted her weight, uncrossed her arms, dropped one hand to her hip, and quirked the side of her mouth up as if she found Clay's monosyllabic banter amusing.

"I don't really have an official rental, but I do have a loaner I could give you until your car is ready. You might not like it though." Clay slowly got up from the scuffed rolling office chair. It squeaked loudly as she stood.

"If it runs and has wheels I'll like it." River followed Clay around the corner to the back of the garage. They stopped next to Clay's 70s era Ford truck. She pulled keys from her pocket and dangled them in River's direction from her finger.

"Is that your truck?"

Clay shrugged.

"Is that a yes?"

"Yes."

"I'm not going to take your truck. What will you drive if I do?"

Clay pointed to a black Moto Guzzi motorcycle parked nearby.

"That's yours too?"

"Yeah, I actually ride that when the weather's nice anyway, so you're welcome to the truck." Clay felt sure River would decline the offer.

"Okay then." River swiped the keys from her fingers and walked toward the truck.

"Uh, it's a stick. It has a three-speed shifter on the column." Clay thought for sure that'd send River packing back to the B and B. In fact, she was looking forward to calling Grace to come pick her up.

"That's no problem. I grew up driving my dad's old truck." River opened the door, slipped off her heels, and tossed them, along with her bag, onto the bench seat of the truck. Then she did this impressive acrobatic move where she hopped butt first up onto the seat then swiveled her legs around. River obviously knew how to maneuver in the tight skirt without giving Clay even the slightest view of anything except her shapely legs sliding sideways onto the seat. River pulled the door closed and cranked the truck, pushing the stick up into reverse.

She rested her elbow through the open window and looked at Clay. "What?"

"Uh…" Clever words, if there were any, never materialized. Was that the distant sound of a phone ringing or was that ringing only inside her head? An alarm sounding perhaps? Signaling that River already had her number, so to speak.

"I didn't grow up in New York City, you know. I'm from Upstate New York…the North Country…farms, cows, and lots of corn." River flashed Clay a brilliant smile and flipped her hair back over her shoulder. "You have my number on that paperwork I signed. If you need the truck back just call me. I'll do my best not to misplace my phone again."

Clay stood silently and watched River pull away…in *her* truck. She never thought for a minute River would actually take it.

Eddie walked over from the open bay door and stood next to her, his frame casting a long shadow.

"Wow." He rubbed the stubble on his chin and whistled.

"Shut up."

"She's as hot as a blacktop in August, and she's not taking any of your shit."

"Shut up," she said it again, not really meaning it. She watched the truck's taillights flame red as River braked and turned left at the intersection.

"Here, a call came in while you were talking to Ms. New York Hottie."

Clay read the scribbled name on the scrap of paper. "Oh, come on."

"Yep, Lynnette's battery is dead again." Eddie wiped his hands on a red bandana he'd pulled from his back pocket. "I'm starting to think she leaves the old Chevy's headlights on just to get you out to the house once a month."

Clay groaned.

"It sucks to be you." Eddie smiled and walked back toward his current work in progress.

Clay strode toward the office.

"Where are you going?"

"I need to make a call before I head to Lynnette's." Clay spun the phone around and sat on the front edge of the desk while she waited for someone to pick up.

"Dispatch, Patsy speaking."

"Patsy, I need to speak to Grace."

"Hold please." Patsy clicked off. After a few seconds of dead air, she was back. "Grace is indisposed. She recommended that if this is an actual emergency you should hang up and dial nine-one-one."

"Patsy, put Grace on the phone or I'm gonna drive over there in person."

"Hold please." Pasty sounded as if she was trying not to laugh. After another brief moment of silence on the line, Grace picked up.

"What's so urgent that I don't have time to put sugar in my coffee?"

"I'd like to report a crime."

"Really?" Grace slurped her coffee loudly.

"Yes, I'd like to report someone who just left the garage and is driving barefoot." A visual flashed of River tossing her heels on the seat just before pulling off that sexy gymnastics maneuver she'd used to get herself and that tight skirt up into the truck.

"Barefoot you say?"

"Yeah, isn't it illegal to drive barefoot?"

Grace snorted. "No. Not in Georgia, not anywhere. That's an urban myth." Grace paused. "Wait a minute, is that River driving your old truck?" Clay could swear she heard the rustling of metal mini blinds from Grace's end of the line.

"That's not funny. You dropped her off knowing we don't have a loaner."

"Visual evidence seems to suggest you do." Grace took another excessively loud sip of coffee. "I assume you confirmed that she has a valid driver's license and insurance?"

"Uh…"

"What's the matter? Were you too distracted by her immense visual charms? She does look pretty hot driving your truck."

"Grace—"

"I simply told Ms. Hemsworth that Cayhill Towing and Auto Repair was a full-service shop. You are, aren't you?"

"What?"

"A full service—"

Clay slammed the phone down. She jerked the trucker cap low over her eyes, crossed her arms, and exhaled loudly. *Dammit all to hell.* She reached for the keys to the tow truck and then stormed out the door.

Chapter Eight

R iver parked Clay's pickup next to a champagne colored BMW sedan with a vanity plate that read RLTYCHK. Either the car belonged to the Realtor she was supposed to meet or the owner was possibly advertising that they needed a reality check. River was certainly feeling as if she needed one after spending twenty-four hours in this steamy small town.

She switched off the engine, slipped on her heels, and stepped out of the truck at the same time as a trim woman with long, perfectly wavy blond hair climbed out of the BMW. This woman had to be Natalie Payne.

"Are you River Hemsworth? I'm Natalie…Natalie Payne. So nice to meet you." Her accent was syrupy sweet as she extended her manicured fingers in River's direction.

"Hello, nice to meet you."

"I love your outfit." Natalie made a slow wave motion with her hand. "Beautiful blouse and your figure is perfection in that skirt."

"Thank you."

"I have to say though, I didn't expect to see you driving that." Natalie quirked an eyebrow and tipped her head toward the old pickup truck. "I suppose that means you've met our local star, Clay Cahill."

"Uh, yes, I had some car trouble yesterday and she loaned me her truck temporarily." Why was Natalie describing Clay as a star? She drove the town's only tow truck. Was that what qualified someone for stardom in Pine Cone? If so, she needed to get back to New York as soon as humanly possible.

"She must like you if she let you drive her truck." Natalie winked and quirked one side of her bright red lips up into a slight smile.

"I'm not sure I'd say that."

"Hmm, sounds like a story I need to hear." Natalie looped her arm through River's. "You can tell me all about it over lunch, after we do our walk through of the property." Natalie Payne was even perkier in person than she'd been over the phone, or email, if that was possible. She followed River into the gallery attached to the house, chatting nonstop. She hardly took a breath.

Natalie obviously felt it was her obligation to give River the entire history of Pine Cone, Georgia. Which River might have appreciated if she planned to stay, but she didn't.

Pine Cone's beginning sounded typical enough. The town sprung up during a time when all you needed was a railroad depot, a cotton gin, or a tobacco auction barn to seed a new community.

"And then before you know it, there's a church, a school, a bank, and a courthouse. And as certain citizens prosper, a golf course and country club become necessary because, obviously, you can't hold the debutante ball in the high school gym." Natalie continued to chatter as she took photos with her phone and made notes on a spiral pad. She'd clearly mastered multitasking on an impressive scale.

River nodded politely and tried to keep up.

"Pine Cone is a mecca for artists too, you know. Art Trails happens every spring where artists and sculptors from all over the community open their studios to the public. People come for miles to buy art and soak up the local culture."

"Really? I had no idea."

"Oh, yes, Interstate 95 is an East Coast corridor that comes within a few miles of the town limits, tourists flock to our little artsy enclave. It's the perfect stopover on their way to vacation in Florida." Natalie sounded like a vacation brochure as she snapped a photo of the crown molding along the back of the gallery space. "Stay here another day or two and you'll see what I mean. There's a big gathering every Wednesday night during the summer for the downtown market. They close Main Street and vendors set up booths. There's food and live music and lots of art." Natalie paused with her hand on her hip. "You own a gallery in New York, right?"

"Yes."

"What's the name?"

"Oh, It's my last name. The Hemsworth Gallery."

"What part of the city is it in? You know, I get to New York at least once a year. I love Broadway. Maybe I could stop in."

"It's near the East Village, a couple of blocks from the Bowery Hotel." River had a hard time picturing Natalie in the Village. She had an even harder time imagining Natalie liking anything hanging on the walls in her small gallery. The exhibits were mostly emerging artists, contemporary in style, and ranged from paints to textiles.

"Sounds cute."

Cute was the absolute last word she wanted to hear anyone use to describe either her gallery or the works displayed on its walls. Natalie was probably the perfect woman to sell this property to a local buyer, but her constant perky conversation was starting to wear on River. She pulled her phone from her bag and glanced at the time, willing the minutes to pass quickly.

River trailed behind Natalie as they left the gallery and walked through her aunt's house. She'd accurately guessed that the house had been built in the late 1940s. It was a simple post WW II brick ranch house floor plan, with three bedrooms and two bathrooms. The home had probably originally had only one bathroom, but her aunt had added a second bath when she built the addition for the gallery. At least that was Natalie's recollection. This would definitely increase the value of the property, according to Natalie. River listened politely as Natalie pointed out details in each room where her aunt had added small touches to the original interior. Built-in bookcases in the living room, pocket doors leading to the master bedroom, and closets built out with shelving to make the best use of a small space. The hardwood floors were narrow tongue and groove pine, darkened from age, but overall in very good condition. The walls were plaster. Each room was a different color. One was a dark red wine color, an interesting choice for the master bedroom. The other two bedrooms were a dark blue-gray, with white crown molding along the ceiling.

The living room walls had white wainscoting halfway up the wall, and then a sea foam green covered the plaster portion to the ceiling. The cool hue on the walls pushed the space out visually, making the room seem larger than it was. River was surprised by how much she approved of her aunt's color scheme. She obviously had a good sense of design and color. River felt a slight tug of guilt at not having known her aunt better. Her father and her aunt had never gotten along, keeping a safe distance from each other even at family funerals and weddings.

After another forty-five minutes, Natalie stowed her spiral notebook in her pink leather handbag. River hoped this was a sign that their time together was drawing to a close.

"Can I treat you to lunch?" Natalie caught River off guard with the question.

"I'd love to, but I feel like I should spend a little time here and...go through things."

"Oh, yes, I'm sorry. You did just arrive. I'm sure you'd like some time alone with your aunt's things."

River nodded. She wasn't sure what she wanted except a little solitude. She definitely wasn't in the mood for lunch and what would no doubt be a hundred personal questions from Natalie Payne.

"Well, I'll leave you to it then. I'll call you later today with my thoughts about how we should price this place and where to advertise. I already have your seller's agreement. We just need to confirm the asking price." Natalie leaned in and touched one cheek to River's, offering up a typical A-frame sorority girl hug. "You have my number. Don't hesitate to ring me if you need anything. I mean it."

River nodded again as she held the door for Natalie. "Thank you."

She leaned against the closed door and let out a long sigh, relieved to have the space to herself. She walked back to the kitchen and set her bag on the center island. She pulled out a large manila envelope that her aunt's attorney had given her. The package had contained keys to the house, the car, and one legal-sized ivory envelope with her name written on the front. With all the commotion the previous day at the crash site, she'd forgotten to open it.

For some reason, she was almost afraid to find out what it said, but that seemed silly. She retrieved a knife from a nearby drawer and neatly sliced open the top of the envelope. Before she had a chance to read it, her phone rang.

❖

Lynette was standing on the porch when Clay pulled the tow truck up. She parked close to the back of the old Chevy Impala and hoisted the portable jump kit from the truck bed. Lynette waved and walked in her direction wearing a tight tank top and cutoff shorts, her tanned legs, long and shapely. Neon pink toenails caught Clay's eye as she crossed the bright green grass. Lynette embraced the old adage that the bigger the hair, the closer to God. And Clay had to admit that the last time she'd been with Lynette the sex had made her call the Lord's name. But today she wasn't in the mood for sex, or flirtation, or anything else. Something about her recent encounters with River rolled around in her empty stomach like a lopsided stone.

She popped the hood and attached the cables determined to focus on the task at hand and nothing else.

"Thanks for coming over, Clay." Lynette touched Clay's shoulder lightly. "You're looking fine today."

"Thank you. You too." Clay glanced sideways and smiled thinly.

"Is something wrong?"

"No, just had a bad morning." Clay straightened and tugged her cap low over her eyes.

"Let me make it better for you." Lynette tugged Clay's hand free from her pocket and held on to it. "I don't have to be at the diner for work until the dinner shift starts at four." She cocked her head playfully and tugged the hairpin free letting her piled tresses fall past her shoulders.

In Clay's opinion, watching a woman's long hair fall in loose waves from a tight knot had to be one of the sexiest visuals on the planet. But even that calculated move wasn't going to work for Lynette today.

"You're sweet." Clay tried to smile and mean it. "I'm no good today. Maybe another time."

"Okay, sugah. I'll take a rain check." Lynette released Clay's hand. "But are you sure there's nothing I can do?"

"Nah, but thanks."

Clay had struggled to find her way back to herself ever since she'd returned to Pine Cone from New York. That had been a few months ago now, and still she couldn't seem to reset her life. Veronica Mann had fucked her, literally and figuratively. Casual sex hadn't helped. A menial job with no stress wasn't helping. Home-cooked meals weren't helping. Time with her besties, Trip and Grace, hadn't even helped. She'd buoy just a little, breaking the surface of her malaise briefly, and then sink again. And she definitely wasn't painting. The naked canvases leaned, stacked along the walls at her place mocking her daily.

Within a half hour, Lynette's Chevy was running and Clay was headed back toward town. It was only around eleven o'clock, but she needed food. She spotted Trip's truck parked at an angle in front of the Dogwood Diner. The tow truck was too big for a standard parking slot so Clay turned into the church parking lot a block away and walked back to the diner. The bell chimed brightly as she pushed through the swinging door. The aroma of a burger on the grill made her stomach growl. She spotted Trip in a booth next to the window.

"Hey there, Clay."

"Hi."

"I'd say you look like you just lost your best friend, but I'm sittin' right here." Trip smiled up at Clay.

"I'll bring a menu over, hon." Jolene waved to Clay from behind the counter near the register.

"No rush." Clay spoke over her shoulder to Jolene. Clay pushed her hat back and rested her elbows on the table.

A quick minute later, Jolene showed up with Trip's omelet in one hand and a menu in the other. The diner served breakfast all day, and that sounded good at the moment. It was still officially morning anyway since it was only eleven o'clock. "You want a coffee?" Clay nodded as she accepted the menu.

"Clay, I expected you to be a little tired, but a happy sort of tired."

"What are you talking about?" Clay looked up from the menu. She wasn't sure why she was even reading it. She always ordered the same thing.

"I called the shop looking for you, and Eddie said you were out at Lynette's place. I know she's carrying a big torch for you." Trip sprinkled hot sauce on her omelet.

"Her battery was dead." Clay frowned.

"And the only thing you jumpstarted was her car? I'm starting to worry about you, friend." Trip took a big bite, smiling around her mouthful of breakfast.

Clay was in the process of constructing a clever retort when the bell over the door rang, distracting her. River paused as the door swished closed behind her. She was looking in Clay's direction but made no move to say hello and neither did Clay. But that didn't stop Trip from waving River over. She swallowed and stood up, motioning for River to join them. Clay tried to signal frantically with her eyes. *No, no, no,* but Trip was clearly not getting the message.

"River, would you care to join us? Clay hasn't even ordered yet, so your timing is perfect." Trip made a gallant show, completely ignoring Clay's glare, extending her arm to the empty half of the bench seat on her side of the table.

"Hi. I wouldn't want to intrude, uh…Trish." River gave Clay a sideways glance, the expression on her face signaled uncertainty, and Clay made no real move to make her feel welcome.

"Trip. Short for Tripoli, but that's a long story. Please join us. I insist. Maybe you can help me cheer up my friend here."

"Oh, yes, Trip. Sorry."

"Completely understandable given the situation, you know, and bouncing your head on the steering wheel and all." Trip was gracious, not making River feel bad for forgetting her name.

Clay was in a bad mood, that was probably obvious, and now Trip had gone and called attention to it in front of River, which annoyed her even further. She was considering her escape when Trip switched sides, moving her plate across the table and sliding into the seat next to Clay, blocking her escape.

"Are you sure I'm not interrupting something?" River seemed to be picking up on Clay's unease.

"Not at all. Please, sit." Trip swiped the menu out of Clay's hand and handed it to River. "They serve breakfast all day and the burgers are good."

"Thank you." River accepted the shiny, tri-folded menu as she slid into the empty bench seat across from them.

"If I'd known I was going to have company I'd have waited to order. Y'all don't mind if I start without you do you? This omelet won't be good if it gets cold."

"Don't wait for us." Clay figured the sooner Trip started eating, the sooner her mouth would be full, and the sooner she'd stop talking.

Trapped, Clay did her best to look everywhere but at River. That was a tall order. River was hard to ignore, and every time she glanced up at Clay, a tiny tingle darted through Clay's innards. She reasoned those twinges were simply hunger pains and ordered eggs with chicken fried steak and sawmill gravy as soon as Jolene came back to take their order. She expected River to order something annoyingly sensible like a green salad and was surprised when River asked for a cheeseburger and fries. First MJ's homemade bread and now this. A beautiful woman who actually liked to eat. Hmm, interesting and unexpected.

"So, River, I overheard you say to Grace that you live in New York City. What line of work are you in?" Trip was infuriatingly curious about River.

Clay already knew the answer to that question. The spinning ceiling fan reflected in the shiny chrome cap of the sugar canister held more interest for her than where this conversation was headed.

"I own an art gallery."

"Really?" Trip took a swig of her sweet tea. "Did you know that Clay is a painter?"

River watched as Clay tilted her head, her eyes shadowed by the brim of her hat, as she glared at Trip.

"What do you paint?" River half expected Clay to say that she painted houses, because aside from the brooding intensity, she didn't really give off an artist vibe.

"I don't paint anything." Her expression signaled that this discussion topic was finished, which made River even more curious.

The food arrived, giving River a few moments to regroup. She daintily hoisted the huge burger and took a bite. Trip had been right. It was great. First fresh baked bread, then hot cinnamon rolls, now this. She was definitely going to have to hit the gym hard when she got back to New York if she kept eating like this.

She looked over at Clay's heaping plate of grays and browns, and before she could stop, she blurted, almost to herself, "I finally get it. There is no chicken in chicken fried steak."

Clay simply stared across the table at her, fork full of battered meat, midair. Trip was laughing so hard she had to dab tears at the corner of her eyes.

"That is the funniest thing I've heard, maybe ever." Trip continued to chuckle in between sips of iced tea.

River felt her Northernism, her otherness, utterly exposed. She swallowed, feeling her cheeks flame under Clay's scrutiny.

"I can't believe I said that out loud."

"I'm so glad you did. That was priceless." There was humor in Trip's words, but no ridicule.

"It's just that I've heard of that dish before, but never quite understood what it was, until now." It seemed so obvious now. Chicken fried steak was simply steak, covered with batter and fried, like chicken.

Trip smiled broadly. "I'm sure some wise person once said, you don't know till you know."

River liked Trip. Her manner was open and friendly. She didn't seem to have a judgmental bone in her body. However, the player vibe was alive and well. Trip would be easy to flirt with and likely fun to date, but River didn't read her as the serious type, and Trip and Clay were obviously friends. Maybe it was true that opposites attract, in friendship as well as in romance. Her shoulders relaxed and she took another bite of her very tasty cheeseburger.

The conversation was pleasant and affable as they continued to eat. River tried to regain her composure after having blurted out something she'd meant for internal monologue. Clay didn't contribute much. Trip did most of the talking about new renovations at her clinic. Trip sounded like someone who loved her work. She was easy to talk with and was clearly doing her best to compensate for Clay's noticeable silence.

"Well, I better get going. Duty calls."

"Oh, so soon?" River wasn't looking forward to finishing her meal while getting the silent treatment from Clay.

"Yep, afraid so. I have to go tend to two of Virginia's prized Friesian mares I'm boarding at the clinic for the final weeks of their pregnancies." Trip dropped a twenty on the table and folded her napkin under the edge of her plate. "Virginia is meeting me there, and it's best not to keep her waiting." She winked at Clay.

Clay swallowed hard and gripped her fork as if her life depended on it as Trip stood to leave. She gave her a look that she hoped said *I'm gonna kill you.* Trip was clearly leaving her stranded with River on purpose. She'd practically inhaled that omelet. This was twice her friends had set her up. First, when Grace dropped River off at the shop for a loaner, and now this. Half eaten chicken fried steak, swimming in gravy, mocked her from the plate, her stomach suddenly south of queasy.

"Catch you later, Paintball."

"Paintball?"

In the background, the bell over the door signaled Trip's exit.

Clay swallowed. "It's a long story."

"Maybe you'll share it sometime."

There was nothing she could do now. She was trapped by her Southern upbringing and her unfinished brunch. Anything less than polite or friendly in this scenario would be an epic fail. She smiled weakly at River. The silence became awkward as River finished her cheeseburger. Jolene scowled curiously at Clay as she refilled her coffee as if she was scolding her for not being more sociable to Pine Cone's newest guest.

"I'm sorry I ruined your meal."

She coughed into her napkin.

"You didn't ruin anything. I'm just not in a very good mood." Now she felt bad.

"Just today? Or ever?" River smiled thinly.

"Most days lately."

River left Clay's response hanging out there.

"So, you're a painter who doesn't paint?"

"Something like that."

"How do you just stop painting?"

"What do you mean?"

"Well, for the artists I've known, creating is almost a compulsion...something they can't stop doing."

"More like an affliction." Clay heard the flat tone of her own voice and hated it. River was right. It hurt almost as much to try to paint as not to paint. She'd stare at a blank canvas for an hour, waiting. Waiting for the veil to lift, waiting for a moment of clarity, waiting for her artistic voice to return, only to be greeted by deafening silence. Her spirit felt caged in a dark place, alone. She sipped her coffee and looked out the window. She felt like crying. What a loser.

"Hey, I didn't mean to upset you again."

River's light touch on her hand surprised her and she flinched.

"What do you mean, again?"

"Well, I obviously upset you in the truck yesterday and you seem upset now."

"I'm not upset. And even if I were it'd have nothing to do with you." She met River's unwavering gaze. She found she couldn't look away. They held each other with their eyes, and an unexpected warmth settled deep inside. *Don't go there. This is how you got in trouble in the first place.* Clay averted her eyes and cleared her throat.

When she looked back, River was still watching her.

Clay reclined against the high back of her seat and sighed.

"Do you ever have such strong feelings about something that there are no words for them?"

River seemed surprised by Clay's question. Her lips parted as if she wanted to say something, but she didn't.

"What if you had only one language to express the unexplainable and that one language was taken away from you?"

"Clay, I didn't—"

"That's why I don't paint." Clay stood and pulled crumpled bills from her pocket and dropped them on the table. "I don't think I'll ever paint again."

She didn't wait for a response from River. She pulled the brim of her hat low and angled quickly for the door. A knot rose in her throat as the door swished closed behind her. Clay shoved her hands in her pockets and strode briskly down the sidewalk to where she'd left the tow truck.

Chapter Nine

By one o'clock, River had checked out of the B and B and by two o'clock was looking through inventory in the back of her aunt's gallery. She assumed that the work stored in narrow wooden slats in the back room were simply paintings waiting for rotation space on the gallery walls. It would be smart to rotate inventory every three months to refresh the space for repeat customers but also to protect the original work from overexposure to sunlight. The space had two large windows at the front and track lighting strategically spaced to highlight various works along each wall.

Most of the paintings in storage were what she'd expect to find in a small, provincial gallery. And although the subject matter was rather pedestrian, the level of craft was high. There were obviously some talented local painters in Pine Cone. Assuming these were from local artists.

There were a few canvases stored at the far end of the space, away from the others for some reason. River slid the first canvas out for a better look. Her breath caught in her chest and she reflexively took a step back. It was almost as if something in the work had physically shoved her. Intimacy clung to the canvas, and River shivered at the thrill of stumbling upon a gem of such authentic artistic vision.

The second painting in this group was equally strong. She placed them side-by-side and stepped away from them for a better look. All together, it seemed there were three paintings by this same artist. River searched the piece for a signature of some kind. She finally found it along the bottom edge of the stretched canvas, on the narrow strip folded around the bottom of the frame.

Surely she'd read the name wrong. River held the canvas bottom side up to the light for a better view. Clayton Cahill was written in dry brush, on all three canvases. Her stomach flipped over on itself. This couldn't mean what she was thinking it meant. There was no way.

Her laptop was in the house. She dug it out of her bag and used her cell phone as a hotspot. It took a moment for the browser to come to life. Searching for *Clayton Cahill, painter* returned a list of results, including images, some of which looked similar to the canvases in her aunt's gallery storage.

She clicked to enlarge the photos, and an image of Clay and photos of her paintings filled the first page of the search. Clay was in a black fitted T-shirt and jeans. Her hair was slightly longer than it was now, but that was definitely her. River squinted to read the caption: *Clayton Cahill in her New York studio.*

"You have got to be fucking kidding me." River bit her lower lip as she pulled up other photos of Clay in her studio, Clay painting, Clay dressed in a dark suit at some gala event with Veronica Mann leaning intimately against her arm.

How had River not connected the dots? She knew Veronica Mann professionally, but didn't really like her. Still, the woman did have impeccable taste, and her gallery was well regarded. She was known for recruiting hot new talent for shows. She was known for bedding those rising stars as well. River's stomach clenched at the thought that a predator like Veronica had gotten her claws into Clay.

River scrolled down the list pulling up reviews of Clay's solo show at the Veronica Mann Gallery.

Critics obviously loved her. They raved like Clay was some sort of lesbian Jackson Pollack. One wrote that Clay painted with candor and perception. That her work was severe and penetrating, with an unnerving harmony of balance and tone. Words like *originality* popped up repeatedly as River read other reviews. *Self-assured, candid, surfaces enlivened with texture and color. Cahill's canvases depict an emotional narrative that engages the viewer beyond the mere surface. A sensitive viewer will find that the work continues to gradually reveal itself upon repeated viewings of the strikingly evocative compositions.*

One critic's interpretation was that Clay had an innate ability to express loss and yearning.

Loss and yearning. Was this the language Clay was trying to describe during their lunch? River sank back into the sofa feeling like a jerk. She'd made a lot of assumptions about Clay, and so far, all of them had been wrong. How had she never crossed paths with Clay in New York? Probably because she avoided Veronica.

River had the overwhelming urge to share this discovery. She reached for her phone and dialed her assistant, Amelia, who picked up almost immediately.

"Hi. When did you get back to the city?" Amelia sounded upbeat.

"Um, I'm not back yet."

"You're still stuck in Georgia?" River could almost hear Amelia's laser focus through the phone.

"Yes and no." River leaned forward, fixed on the artistically cropped black-and-white photo of Clay standing in her New York studio. "Are you near your laptop?"

"Yes, why?"

"Google Clayton Cahill."

"Okay, is there a reason I'm looking up this guy…oh, not a guy."

"No, definitely not a guy."

"Clayton Cahill, the painter. And P.S. completely gorgeous."

"Okay, focus." River knew Amelia wasn't even interested in women, but the comment still triggered some small sliver of protectiveness. "Are you looking at the review in the *Times*?"

"Yeah, they love her work." Amelia was quiet for a moment except for the clicking of computer keys. "This is a very positive review for a first solo exhibit. So, why am I caring about Clayton Cahill?"

"Because Clay is here."

"In Pine Cone, Georgia?" The pitch of Amelia's voice notched up.

"My aunt had a few of Clay's pieces in her gallery storage. I came across them today." River paused. "Listen, I need to stay here for at least another week, maybe two."

"Two?"

"If I could convince Clay to let us represent her work… maybe even do a show…this could be really great for the gallery. We'd instantly be on the radar of every major reviewer in New York. This could finally give us the attention we need." River tried to temper her excitement. "Amelia, this could be big for us."

"I get it. I agree with you. I'm just sensing there's a *but* in there somewhere."

"At the moment, Clay isn't painting."

"A painter who no longer paints? How's that going to help us?"

"Leave that to me." River closed her laptop and leaned back. "Can you handle things while I'm away?"

"Sure, no problem."

"And wish me luck."

"Good luck, River." Amelia paused. "Although, I'm not sure you'll need it. You are lethally irresistible. I don't know how anyone, including this Clay Cahill, could possibly resist you if there's something you really want."

"Thanks for the vote of confidence."

"Don't mention it, boss."

River clicked off. She felt excited and restless. Maybe she needed to go for a run and burn off some energy. A long run would also help her think. She closed the laptop and headed toward the bedroom to change into shorts, but a photo on the wall in the long narrow hallway caught her eye. She stepped closer. There was a black-and-white image of her aunt with her arm around a much younger version of Clay, probably in her early teens.

The hallway was full of small personal photos. River had walked past them a few times but hadn't stopped to really study them. Now she saw that there was a whole group that included Clay. Was it possible that her aunt had been a mentor to Clay?

The letter. She looked back toward the brightly lit kitchen. The letter from her aunt was still lying on the kitchen counter. She'd opened it earlier, but her phone had rung before she'd gotten to read it. And then she'd forgotten because her friend Jillian had been in crisis and had kept her on the phone forever. She'd gone to the diner and then back to the B and B to check out and forgotten the envelope.

River leaned against the counter as she pulled the folded ivory paper free of the envelope.

Dear River,

If you're reading this letter, then I missed the opportunity to share any of this with you in person, and for that, I'm truly sorry. I have many regrets in my life, and not knowing you may be the biggest one of them. It was your father's wish that I have little or no contact with you, because of the choices I've made. I have honored that request. But as you get older, you realize the social constraints we set for ourselves and accept from others are sometimes cruel and unnecessary. And time wasted cannot be recaptured.

Reflexively, River dropped onto a nearby kitchen stool. The contents of the letter felt more personal than she'd expected.

Your father is a good man, and as my only brother, I loved him. But I let him keep me from getting to know you. Once I realized I had feelings for women, that I was a lesbian, I left home and made a life for myself elsewhere.

Like many women of my era, I married young, right out of high school. David Gardner was a nice man and a fine person, but I could not make him happy because I was not happy. Your father thought I should have stayed in the marriage, made it work, overcome my desires for a different life. Obviously, I made a choice not to do that. David and I separated after two years, and I could not stay in Canton.

I think your father was afraid my choices would influence you or your brother in some way. He didn't believe in divorce, and he certainly did not understand what it was like to be a lesbian.

Imagine how proud I was to read of your successes in New York. If I'd been well enough, oh how I would have loved to visit you there and see your gallery. But if you are reading this, then I waited too long. Your father is gone, and now I am gone and you will only have the words of this letter to tell you the truth of it all.

Your mother was a kind woman, a generous woman, and she wrote letters and sent photos all along. I was able to feel at least a little part of your life, even if it was from a distance.

River wiped at a tear on her cheek as she shuffled the paper to read the second page.

Please don't be angry with your father or with me. Times were different. We lived in a conservative rural community. I left there when I could hide my true self no longer, and I never returned. Luckily, I eventually found a new community here. One that would support me throughout the rest of my life. I found love here and friendships, and I discovered my love of art, our shared passion.

You may decide to sell the house and the gallery. Feel free to do whatever suits you. Everything is now yours to do with as you wish. There are only three paintings I hope you will not sell. They were done by a local artist named Clay Cahill. Those I would like for you to keep or return to Clay. They are the only ones of real value to me. And knowing what I know of the shows you've curated in New York, I think you might like them. The details for how to contact her are in the ledger in the gallery. I have contact info for all the artists whose work I've shown should you be curious.

I've tried to make peace with my regrets. I'm a frail, old woman now. If I might give you some advice that I've learned from the mistakes I've made it would be, live your own life.

Live it fully, live it fearlessly, and live it for love.

—Eve Gardner

River let the pages rest on the countertop. The final line of the letter bringing tears to the edge of her lashes unexpectedly.

She loved her mother and father, but she'd always known they struggled with her sexuality. Her brother was completely at home in small town America. He never chafed at the restrictions her parents had placed on them as kids. But she had. And in her teens she'd begun to realize she was a lesbian.

Her father had struggled with that. Even as an adult, he'd always referred to her lovers as *friends*. As if he could never bring himself to accept fully who she was. Now some of that made sense. He'd had his own personal struggle that he'd never shared with her. How could he? And yet, if he had, things might have made more sense.

River thought of her mother. Her mother had obviously felt it was important not to completely isolate Eve from the family. And maybe on some level her mother had thought Eve would be, could be, a mentor for her. Now, like so many other times when she had something to share, she missed her mother. She wanted nothing more than to be able to talk to her mother, but she'd died a few years before her father, no doubt hastening his decline.

Slowly, she surveyed the contents of the house, every small item now taking on new significance and meaning.

CHAPTER TEN

Clay drove back to the garage, planning to fill the rest of her day with mindless mundane tasks. She didn't want to think about blank canvases waiting to be filled. She didn't want to think about that luminous patch of existence she'd left behind in New York, that moment of glory. And she most certainly did not want to think about River Hemsworth.

Willing time to pass quickly was more difficult than she'd imagined. The afternoon seemed to drag on forever. Customers stopped in for gas or a soda. Her grandpa had never updated to automated pumps. In fact, these pumps were so old they only showed the cents. They'd been installed during an era when not as many digits were required. A time when it would have been absurd to think a gallon of gas would cost even a dollar. There was a handwritten sign on both pumps adding two dollars to the price that showed on the pump. Locals knew this of course, but tourists were always amused by the vintage pumps and the price per gallon, a throwback to simpler times before cell phones and Twitter and reality TV hosts thinking they could be president.

She lingered in the front office, near the register, taking her time to restock the drink cooler and replenish the candy bar display.

"I gotta drive over to Andy's and pick up some parts." Eddie talked to Clay through the open door from the shop.

She nodded.

"Bo is working on that Pontiac. At a snail's pace." He muttered the last part under his breath.

Clay nodded again with a frown and leaned over so that she could see Bo past Eddie's shoulder.

"You might want to check on him after I leave."

"I will, although a lot of good that'll do. He pretty much ignores me." It didn't seem to matter to Bo that Clay's grandpa owned the place. He tolerated her, and that was about it. The sooner he was gone the better she'd sleep at night.

She waited about twenty minutes before she nonchalantly took a stroll through the triple bay garage. Bo was nowhere near the Pontiac he was supposed to be working on. She heard a scuffling sound from the back storage room and headed in that direction. Before she reached the door, Bo suddenly appeared. He had a sheepish expression, a new look for him, as if he'd been up to something and she'd almost caught him.

He took several long strides toward the raised hood of the Pontiac. His mousy light brown hair was pressed to his head by sweat and humidity. Some might have thought his pupils were misdirected, but in reality, he was simply shifty and rarely made eye contact. A physical feature that only added to Clay's distrust of him.

"You almost finished here? I'd like to give the owner a call by the end of the day with the status." She crossed her arms and attempted to make herself taller.

"It's comin' along." He shrugged.

"Does that mean I should call them to pick it up before we close?"

"Probably not till tomorrow." He seemed to have no sense of urgency about either the customer or the repair or her questions about his progress.

If she owned the garage, she'd have fired him right on the spot. She was sure he was taking twice as long to do the repair which was basically replacing hoses and plugs.

"What were you doing back there?" She tipped her head in the direction of the small dark storage area. Not that she thought he'd tell her what he was up to, but she was compelled to ask.

"I was looking for a wrench. I thought I might've left it back there."

His answer sounded plausible and fishy at the same time. She decided to drop it for now.

Clay walked outside and took a few spins around the front parking area to let off steam. Just having to look at his shifty, unshaven face set her off. It was even worse when she had to interact with him or needed something from him. She suspected that he didn't like gay people. He'd called her a *damn dyke* more than once in high school when he didn't think she could hear him. Probably because she had better luck with girls than he did.

She was grateful that mostly Eddie was Bo's direct supervisor in the shop, because her grandpa was rarely around these days. He'd come in the morning for a couple of hours but then manage to disappear in the afternoon. He was definitely leaning to part-time retirement.

Clay slid a bottled Coke out of the cooler and popped the top. She took a long swig and sank into the old rolling chair behind the desk and surveyed the room. A room she'd been in a million times but hardly took time to notice. The whole place could be a set for a movie. Perfectly vintage calendars that had not been replaced in twenty years hung along the wall behind the desk. Probably because her grandpa or Eddie liked the images of the women in bikinis lounging across car hoods. She didn't blame them, although she was surprised the calendars and posters had survived the past decade of political correctness.

One of the models reminded her of River. Long legs, dark hair, lithe, subtly curvaceous with a confident smile. A swirl of heat ignited in her stomach and spread. She held the cool soda bottle to her cheek for a minute.

Clay walked to the drink cooler, opened the swinging glass door, and stuck her whole head inside. She lingered there until the glass fogged up completely, which is why she didn't notice Bo standing in the doorway giving her a curious, unfriendly look.

"What?" The door closed with a swish.

"The Pontiac is ready if you want to make the call."

"Thanks."

A little unbalanced from being caught cooling off by Bo, Clay bumped the ancient spiral magazine rack near the front window. Populated with sun-faded periodicals, the most recent of which was *Time* magazine from six months ago. This was the perfect place to hide out because it seemed immune to the passage of time. But not immune to reminders of River, apparently.

Clay glanced up at the dingy wall clock over the door. Bo wasn't the only thing that moved at a snail's pace. Time in the shop, life in Pine Cone, traveled at the speed of a creeping glacier.

Just before four o'clock, Mrs. Eldridge's plump silhouette filled the doorway. Mrs. Eldridge had been Clay's third grade teacher and had long ago retired. But as always, she was dressed as if she had a very important meeting with the school superintendent. Her white hair tightly curled around her face, her blouse and skirt neatly pressed, and her pudgy feet stuffed into sensible low-heeled pumps.

"Hello, Mrs. Eldridge. What can I do for you?" Clay stood up and walked around the counter from the register.

"Hello, Clayton. The Bonneville is making a funny noise. I was hoping Eddie could have a look. My George always took care of the car, rest his soul, and I'm afraid something terrible is wrong." Her husband had passed on about ten years earlier. Died quietly in his sleep.

"Eddie ran to pick up something, but he'll be back within a half hour. I'll pull the car into the bay so he can take a look first thing when he gets back."

Mrs. Eldridge handed her large bundle of keys to Clay as they walked toward the 90s era powder blue road yacht. It was Clay's habit to take a visual survey of a vehicle before she parked it in the repair bay. She circled the car but stopped dead in her tracks when she reached the rear right wheel. Mrs. Eldridge was clutching her handbag, watching pensively from the other side of the car as if she expected the worst.

"Do you see something?"

"Mrs. Eldridge, what sort of noise is the car making?"

"Whenever I accelerate, it starts to make this thumping sound. The faster I go the more rapid it bangs."

"I may have discovered what is causing the banging noise. Your tires are so badly worn that the steel cords are showing, and it seems that one of them hooked a sock." Clay covered her mouth with her hand so as not to burst out laughing. She was looking down at the disintegrating tire where at the end of the cord hung a dirty, tattered red-ringed tube sock.

Mrs. Eldridge scurried to the far side of the car and stood next to Clay.

"Well, I'll be." She acted astounded as if Clay had discovered the most miraculous thing. Like a cure for cancer.

"I think when you pick up speed the sock thumps against the inside of the wheel well."

"I never thought to walk around to this side of the car." The passenger side of the car might as well have been on the dark side of the moon as far as Mrs. Eldridge was concerned.

"Don't feel bad. This could happen to anyone." Although for the life of her, Clay couldn't imagine who. "I'll check and see if we have tires in stock. I think you need all four replaced." This tire had hardly any rubber left and the other three were almost as bad.

"Dear me." She dabbed at perspiration on her rosy cheeks with a linen handkerchief. "Maybe I'll just leave the car and call my sister to come pick me up."

"That's probably a good idea since it's pretty close to the end of the day."

They walked back to the office where the air conditioner that hung slightly askew in the window strained to cool the room. By the time Eddie returned, Mrs. Eldridge's sister had arrived to rescue her.

As River suspected, her aunt's car wasn't worth repairing. The insurance adjuster called to relay the news. It was just as well. She'd probably have ended up selling the car anyway so the insurance payout would save her the trouble. Hopefully, she could negotiate to keep Clay's truck for the remainder of her stay in Pine Cone. That would be one headache off her to-do list.

Clay? Every time River was around Clay, she was more confused. Did Clay simply not like her? Clay had opened up just the tiniest bit at the end of their lunch at the diner, but then shut down almost immediately.

Regardless of whatever else was going on, River decided to call the garage and ask about keeping the truck. She was reading way too much connection into a loaner car. She shook her head at her own silliness. The rumpled paperwork from the day she'd crashed the car was in the very bottom of her large purse. Everything had to be excavated and piled onto the counter to find it. Seriously, did anyone need this many lipsticks?

The number for Cahill Towing was at the top of the wrinkled form. Her finger hovered over the call button on her phone, but before she could touch it someone knocked at the front door. River opened the door to find an elderly, silver haired woman dressed as if she were on her way to church, standing on her doorstep holding a casserole dish.

"Hello." River leaned lightly against the edge of the open door.

"Hello, dear. I'm Lucille Witmark, a neighbor of Eve's." The woman smiled up at her through vintage lavender cat eye glasses, bedazzled at the corners with sparkly clear stones.

"Hi, Mrs. Witmark. I'm Eve's niece, River."

"It's so nice to meet you, dear. I figured you must be a family member when I saw you here with the Realtor. And please, call me Lucille." Her expression grew suddenly serious. "I'm so sorry for your loss. Losing Eve was a loss to us all, frankly. She was a fine woman and a good neighbor all these many years."

River realized she'd kept Lucille standing on the stoop in the late afternoon heat.

"Please come in." River motioned for Lucille to enter. She was puzzled about the dish covered with a blue plaid towel, but she didn't ask.

"Do you mind if I set this on the counter?" Lucille raised the dish a little in River's direction.

"Yes, of course. I should have asked to take that for you."

"It's no trouble." Lucille removed the covering to reveal some sort of baked casserole with a crumb topping. "This is still warm if you want to have some now. I worried you might not be set up for cooking or forget to eat altogether. That can happen after the loss of a loved one."

"That smells...good. What is it?" River tried to act excited, but she couldn't quite identify the sweet smell wafting from the dish and was almost afraid to ask.

"This is my special pineapple casserole. The Ritz Crackers brown nicely because of the butter and then there's shredded cheddar cheese underneath."

She proudly relayed the partial list of ingredients, while River fought to keep her expression neutral. The combination Lucille had just described sounded terrible.

"Hmm, that sounds delicious."

"Should I serve you a little helping in a dish, honey?"

"Oh, no, I'm not quite hungry yet, but thank you." River glanced at the wall clock in the kitchen and realized it was almost the dinner hour. She'd lost track of time looking through her aunt's things.

"I'll be happy to jot down the recipe for you, dear."

"Oh, thank you, maybe another time?"

"Well, that's probably a good idea. I don't want to be late. I'm off to play bridge down at the Methodist Church. Now you be sure and eat it while it's still warm. It won't be good once the cheese gets hard." Lucille slid her short purse strap up to the crook of her arm. "And if you need anything you just give a shout. I live two doors down. Look for the house with the ladybug mailbox."

Of course, Lucille had a ladybug mailbox. That went along with the rest of the adorable package.

"Thank you so much." River followed Lucille to the door and waved as she walked to her late model sedan parked at the curb in front of the house. It was sort of hilarious to see Lucille's diminutive frame drive off in the huge auto. She appeared to be swallowed up by it and could probably hardly see above the steering wheel.

River returned to the casserole and regarded it suspiciously. Curiosity and hunger pangs got the better of her. She fished a spoon out of a nearby drawer and scooped out the teeniest portion. Timidly, she nibbled a bit off the end of the spoon. Then she tasted a bit more. She scooped out a larger bite and chewed the savory-sweet mixture. Pineapple casserole was pretty darn good. Ten minutes earlier, she didn't even know such a thing existed, and now she was tempted to sit down and eat a good portion of it with a spoon right from the baking pan.

The sugar rush kicked in a dozen mouthfuls later. River glanced up at the clock again and decided to make a quick trip to the market for something green to balance out the dessert casserole that she was quickly consuming.

Chapter Eleven

The Piggly Wiggly was busy with after-work shoppers. The only empty spot River could find was an angled slot out front marked twenty-minute parking for loading. She didn't need much and would surely be in and out in less than twenty minutes, so she pulled in.

The automatic door slid sideways, and the inside cooled air hit her like an arctic blast. The store's interior seriously felt like a meat locker. She wielded a small shopping cart quickly through the produce section and then headed for the cheese counter. Now she just needed to find artisan crackers and sparkling water. Artisan crackers turned out to be missing in action so she settled for a box of Ritz Crackers. *When in Rome.* Amused with herself, she tossed a second box in her cart for good measure, rounded the end of the aisle, and almost bumped into MJ.

"Why, hello there." MJ's cart was completely full.

"Hi." River pulled her cart up alongside MJ's.

"That's hardly what I'd call groceries. No wonder you stay so slim."

River looked down at her carefully selected produce, cheese wedge, and crackers. MJ was right. This was more appetizer than actual substance for a meal. The truth was that River loved to graze on small bites. She wasn't much of a cook.

"I don't expect to be here much longer. These are simply a few things to tide me over." If she stayed in the South for very long, River was figuring out that she'd have to get used to everyone offering their unsolicited opinion.

Before MJ could reply, a sickening stench wafted in their direction. River was so caught off guard by it that she reacted without thinking, scrunching up her nose and covering her mouth. MJ leaned sideways to look past River and down the long aisle.

"Hm-mm." MJ shook her head with a knowing expression on her face.

River turned and saw a woman with tousled light brown hair walking leisurely down the aisle in their direction. Her tan work pants were tucked into high rubber boots covered with dry mud. Her plaid flannel shirt was faded and two sizes too large. As she drew near, River realized that she was the source of the noxious odor. And if she was aware of that fact herself, she gave no indication that she cared one way or the other.

"Birdie, you smell like a skunk." MJ spoke as Birdie's cart came up alongside them.

"I reckon I do."

"And you didn't think to spare the rest of us?" MJ braced a hand on her hip.

"A woman's gotta eat ain't she? I'd starve waitin' for the smell to fade."

"I could've brought something by for you."

"Too much trouble." Birdie reached between River and MJ for a can of tomato soup. "If folks is too fragile to stand the smell of nature, then there's no help for 'em."

"Well, there's the smell of nature and then there's the smell of a skunk. I daresay I prefer one and not the other."

The stench was beginning to make River's eyes water. It coated her throat so that she had to ward off a coughing fit.

"Do you mean you actually got sprayed by a skunk?" The question, which sounded ludicrous when voiced aloud, had escaped before River could stop herself.

Birdie seemed to notice River for the first time. She stared at her with the soup can still in her hand. Not a polite, quick appraisal, more of a laser-focused, melt your core kind of look.

"Why, no, this is my expensive perfume. It's imported. Don't you like it?"

"I, um…"

"Of course, I got sprayed by a skunk. Are you challenged in some way? Are you one of those people who can't recognize smells?"

"That's face blindness you're thinkin' of. It doesn't apply to smells." MJ had come to River's rescue, or tried to.

"And who is you anyway?" Birdie dropped the soup loudly into her cart as she stared River down.

"I'm River…River Hemsworth."

"This is Eve's niece." MJ jumped in. "She's here to settle Eve's affairs."

"Is she now?" Birdie gave River an up and down look. "Well, I'm sorry for yer loss. Eve was a fine person in my opinion, and there aren't many of them left."

MJ nodded in agreement.

River had been trying to breathe through her mouth the whole time, but still the skunk smell was beginning to seep into her pores. Shoppers were cutting a wide path around them. The entire center of the store was clear of customers except for River, MJ, and Birdie.

"Well, I reckon I'll get on out of here before the store manager runs me off." She nodded good-bye and wheeled her squeaky cart to the first available checkout. Bag boys ran for the exit. River felt sorry for the young woman ringing her up. She stretched as far away as possible while still being able to run items past the bar code scanner.

River and MJ headed to the far end of the aisle in an attempt to get past the cloud of skunk that hung in the air. River pushed her cart next to the open freezer case and leaned into the chilled air before she took a breath.

"Welcome to country living."

"How does she stand it?" River braced her hands on the cold case and considered adding some chocolate ice cream to her collection of snacks.

"She's probably used to it. This happens at least once a year." MJ leaned against the case, clearly waiting for Birdie to leave the building before continuing to shop. "She sets traps for rabbits to keep them out of her garden. She doesn't kill them. For all her gruffness, Birdie's an old softy on the inside. Anyway, she takes 'em out in the woods and turns 'em loose. But every now and then she catches a skunk instead of a rabbit."

River reached for a pint of Dutch chocolate.

"Well, I better finish my shopping. I still have chores back at the B and B before my day is at an end." MJ smiled at River as she eased her cart down the next aisle. "Nice to see you, River."

"Nice to see you also."

After another ten minutes of quick turns down a few more aisles, River had a bag in each arm and was heading toward the truck. She came up short when she saw Officer Jamie Grant standing near the driver's side door, scribbling on a small pad.

"I'm here, Officer. I'm just leaving," River called to Jamie from about ten feet away.

Jamie glanced up as she tore the sheet off the pad and slid it under the windshield wiper.

"Seriously?" River hurriedly stowed the groceries on the passenger side and then rounded the front of the truck. Jamie watched her with a neutral expression.

"Ms. Hemsworth, this is a loading zone."

"I know it's a loading zone. But I'm sure I wasn't in the store for more than twenty minutes. The sign says twenty-minute parking."

"You were in the store for thirty-five minutes." Jamie closed the flip cover over the pad and turned toward her squad car. "Feel free to mail the ticket in if you don't have time to go by the courthouse and pay it in person."

Unbelievable. Skunked and ticketed and all she had to show for it was chocolate ice cream and Ritz Crackers. The joy of small town life was wearing thin if it had ever existed in the first place.

Clay was ready to take off for the day. It was after five, and she was itching to get on her motorcycle and ride. She needed to clear her head. But Bo was still lurking in the dark recesses of the garage. Eddie had to leave a little early for his niece's soccer match, which left Clay to babysit Bo. She weaved around a rolling toolbox strewn with a haphazard array of socket wrenches. She didn't see Bo, but the sound of metal clinking pulled her to the far corner of the garage. This was the second time today he'd gone MIA, skulking around for no good reason. She wasn't really in the mood to search for him in the dark storage room.

"Bo, are you still here?" The metallic scuttling sound issuing from the storage room could've been a giant rat, or Bo. She figured it was a toss-up.

He stepped out of the doorway, wiping his hands as if he'd actually been working on something. Clay knew better, she figured he was casing tools to see what he could walk out with in his pockets. She seriously didn't trust him as far as she could throw him. And considering Bo was about the same size as her, that wasn't very far. He was the same surly loser she'd known in grade school.

"I'm ready to close up. Are you finished for the day?"

"Yeah, I reckon I'm done." He stuffed the rag in the back pocket of his sagging jeans. He had a slight beer gut, but no ass to hold up the seat of his pants.

"I'll lock up the front office if you close the bay doors."

He nodded and shuffled toward the nearest large retractable door as if his legs were mired in deep mud. The chain ground against the pulley as he tugged. The sound of metal on metal echoed across the concrete floor and bounced off the cinder block walls. Clay waited in the open front door as he closed the last bay door and switched off the overhead fluorescent lights.

She watched him as he crossed the parking area to his barely legal Toyota truck. The truck had a lift kit, oversized off-road tires, large amorphous spots of unpainted primer, and a roll cage around where doors used to be. The entire rig looked like a castoff reject from the set of the original 1979 Mad Max movie.

Clay swung her leg across the seat of her bike but waited until his beater truck disappeared down the street before she slid her helmet on and cranked the V-twin engine. In her opinion, the transverse cylinder heads that projected prominently on either side made the Moto Guzzi's design unique and singularly badass. Every ounce of thrust between her legs was a much-needed confidence boost after dull hours at the garage spent thinking way too much about things she couldn't change or things she wished she'd done differently.

The motorcycle had been a gift to herself for selling her first painting to a commercial gallery. She was barely eighteen and had decided she was old enough to make potentially unsafe vehicle choices if she wanted to, much to her mother's displeasure. Her grandpa understood. He'd been a gearhead since he was old enough to hold on to a steering wheel so she'd come by her love of all things motorized honestly. Trip had driven down to Florida with her to pick it up. She'd gotten a great deal on the used Guzzi California, all sleek retro, black and chrome. It took every penny of four summers of work at her grandpa's garage, every cent of graduation gift money, and the money she'd earned from selling the painting. And she'd still had to borrow extra from her grandpa, a secret they'd yet to reveal to her mother. Clay had considered upgrading since then, but the newer model Guzzis had lost a bit of charm from her perspective. They were too big and they had too much crap on them. The California was the bike for her. A long ride on this bike was the best therapy money could buy. Money couldn't buy happiness, but it could buy a motorcycle, and the Guzzi certainly brought unparalleled joy.

The crumpled Mercedes caught her eye as she was about to pull out, and her mind traveled to River again. Maybe she should swing by and find out if the insurance company had delivered any news about a settlement. That would be the neighborly thing to do and a professional courtesy seeing as how she'd been the one to tow River's car away. The fact that River had intermittently invaded her thoughts ever since lunch had nothing to do with it. Maybe seeing River would help clear her head. Something about the lunch conversation had stayed with her; she couldn't quite shake it.

Her two-tone Ford truck was parked in Eve's driveway. It was strange to see her truck there and know that River had been driving it. Clay had a flash mental image of driving the truck herself with River next to her on the bench seat, River's thigh touching hers, the smell of her hair, and Clay's arm around her shoulder. Butterflies ensued.

Calm down, Cahill.

Clay killed the ignition and ran her fingers through her hair to revive it.

Chapter Twelve

River froze in front of the large living room window when she saw Clay ease up to the curb and remove her helmet. Like some lesbian fantasy butch dream date, River watched as Clay ran her fingers through her hair and crossed the lawn with long, easy strides. River looked down, suddenly aware that she was wearing gym shorts and a scooped neck T-shirt. Did she have time to change? The doorbell rang. No, she didn't have time to change, and why was she getting all worked up about Clay anyway? Regardless of how hot Clay was in boots, perfectly faded Levi's, and an ab-hugging charcoal T-shirt, she had clearly given River signs repeatedly that she was *not* interested. The more pressing question was if Clay wasn't interested, then why was she here?

"Hello."

"Hi." Clay swept her fingers through her hair again. "Um, I was just leaving work, and thought I'd check to see if you'd heard anything from the insurance company about Eve's car?" She shifted her stance and studied River. The focus of those shadowed dark eyes rippled through River's stomach like successive seismic shock waves.

"Yes, the adjuster phoned this afternoon. I was planning to call you tomorrow about it."

"Oh, all right then." Clay looked down at the ground and then up at River as if she might say something else. She took a half step backward.

"Would you like to come in?" Clay didn't answer right away. A moment's hesitation that made River second-guess the invitation. "No pressure, I just thought—"

"Sure. I mean, if you're not busy."

"I actually just returned from getting a few groceries. I was about to open a bottle of wine if you'd like to join me." River did the math in her head quickly. Clay Cahill and alcohol in the house at the same time, probably not the smartest idea given how River's libido spiked every time she was in close proximity to Clay. Oh, well, too late now.

She stepped aside to allow Clay to enter. Clay set the helmet on the island in the kitchen and casually leaned back against the edge of it. River took a bottle of red wine from the grocery bag. She hoped her aunt had a corkscrew because she hadn't thought to pick one up at the store. The liquor store around the corner from the market had a surprisingly sophisticated selection of wine. She'd been able to find a bottle of a biodynamic wine from Northern California. A Merlot from Benziger. She held the dark bottle in one hand and began opening random kitchen drawers with the other.

"Want me to open that?" Clay pushed off the counter's edge and pulled a corkscrew from the drawer nearest where she stood.

Clay obviously knew her aunt's kitchen better than River did. Given the photos hanging in the hallway, River should have anticipated that.

"Thank you."

Clay took the bottle from River. She gripped the long neck of the bottle with one hand as she worked on retracting the cork with the other. The lean muscles of her tanned forearms flexed as she worked the cork free. River studied Clay's hands. She had a strong desire to run her thumb over the back of Clay's hand, to trace her fingertips along Clay's palm, and up her arm. A woman with strong hands, long fingers, this was one of River's weaknesses. She cleared her throat and busied herself finding glasses before Clay noticed she was staring. Yes, alcohol and Clay were definitely a recipe for bad choices.

Clay poured wine for each of them. River swirled the deep red around in the glass before she sampled it. The Merlot had layers of blackberry, blueberry, and ripe plum with a very nice finish. She couldn't help smiling.

"That's very good." Clay took a second sip.

"I agree."

An awkward silence descended for a moment before River remembered her snack run to the Piggly Wiggly.

"Are you hungry? I picked up cheese and crackers and… um, mostly I just have cheese and crackers." River fished in the brown shopping bag. "Oh, and chips." She proudly held up a bag of BBQ kettle chips.

Clay was amused by River's culinary display, or lack thereof. River clearly hadn't planned on feeding anyone but herself, and now Clay felt bad for showing up unannounced. But unless Clay was completely off her game, River seemed happy to see her. River looked like the poster girl for sexy gym wear. The scooped neck T-shirt she was wearing dipped low enough to reveal a tantalizing hint of cleavage, and the running shorts gave a maximum view of her toned legs. Once again, River was barefoot. For some reason, this amused Clay and she couldn't help smiling.

"What's funny? Oh, wait, you don't have an allergy to dairy do you?" River's crestfallen expression was bookended by the wedge of cheese and the box of crackers she held in each hand.

"No, it's not that." Clay tipped her head toward the floor. "I've been around you only a few times, but you're almost always shoeless. I was just wondering what's at the root of your aversion to shoes." She grinned as she sipped her wine.

River glanced down and then she smiled too. When she looked back up, her eyes sparkled. Clay decided that this casual, girlish version of River Hemsworth was completely enchanting.

"If you'd ever seen my closet you wouldn't ask such a question. I love shoes, as many shoes as possible, but I also love any excuse to take them off." She cocked her head as if she was thinking some deep thought. "You don't have an aversion to toes or something do you? Or some strange foot fetish that I should know about?"

Clay snorted a laugh. "No, absolutely not. Your toes are adorable."

As soon as the compliment escaped her lips, Clay felt her cheeks flame hotly. She felt exposed by the innocent compliment, as if River could see the unvoiced attraction hiding behind it. She wondered if River sensed her discomfort. Clay shoved her free hand in her pocket and busied herself looking everywhere but at River while River sliced cheese and piled crackers on a plate next to the neatly arranged slices.

"Shall we sit?" River motioned toward the sofa.

Clay nodded. How had this turned into a social visit? She'd had every intention of simply stopping by to check in, or so she'd told herself. Now she was joining River on the couch for wine and appetizers as if they were friends. She was suddenly nervous about where this might be headed. The softness of the sofa surrounded her as she dropped to a seated position. Was she leaning back too far? Were her legs too far apart? Her shins grazed the coffee table so she angled sideways a little. Clay smiled thinly around a mouthful of red wine. The Merlot was strong and full-bodied and was going straight to her head. Maybe cheese and crackers were a good idea after all. She'd always been sort of a lightweight on an empty stomach.

She reached for the food and tried to ignore the fact that River was studying her from the other side of the couch. River was angled sideways into the far end of the sofa, her legs tucked discreetly under her so that her abbreviated running shorts didn't give too much away.

"So, I was a little surprised to discover that you used to live in New York City."

Clay didn't remember if she'd mentioned that she lived in New York. She didn't think she had. Had River looked her up? She leaned forward, debating whether to leave.

"I'm sorry, I shouldn't have blurted that out." River shifted as if she were about to reach for Clay, but then she let her hand drop. "I found your paintings in my aunt's gallery and I googled you. I apologize. I promise I'm not a stalker or anything."

Clay exhaled and dropped back, slouching into the deep cushions. If River had googled her, then she probably knew all about Veronica and about the solo show.

"I'm sorry, I didn't mean to pry. When I saw your work I sort of couldn't help myself." River studied her over the rim of her wine glass. "You're a gifted painter."

"Thank you." Clay downed a mouthful of wine, focusing on River's initial comment. "I suppose I always wanted New York, but I'm not sure I was ready for it."

"What do you mean?" River seemed more relaxed now that Clay wasn't poised to bolt for the door.

"Well, if you're going to be serious about art you pretty much have to go to New York City, don't you? I wanted to prove to myself I could make it there, that I could succeed there." Clay sighed. "But New York is tough, maybe even more so when you succeed."

"Where did you study art?"

"Wheaton."

"That's a great school."

"Yeah, I really enjoyed college." Clay reached for a slice of cheese and swallowed before continuing. "I sort of wish I'd studied more, but..." Her voice trailed off because she didn't really want to get into the whole *how I came out* discussion, especially not right now with River.

"Girls?" River teased her.

"Maybe a topic for another time."

"Speaking of girls, or I should say, women...Veronica Mann...she curated your solo show, right?"

River had definitely googled her public life in New York. Clay couldn't decide whether to be annoyed or flattered.

"Wow, you really know how to go right for the sore subject."

"Oh, I'm sorry. We can talk about something else. I was just curious." River reached for a few crackers and held them in her fingers as if she'd been dealt a hand of cards. She nibbled from the corners. "I know her professionally, and I suppose I wondered how well you knew her."

River was plainly fishing for details. The wine or the soft cushions or both were coaxing Clay to relax. Relaxing made her inclined to share. Why not talk to River about what had happened in New York? Maybe talking about it would help. This could be like therapy with a stranger. She and River didn't really know each other, and it wasn't like Clay had any intentions of ever going back to New York City. River was in the same profession as Veronica. Maybe she could shed some light on things, on how Clay could have judged everything so wrongly.

"I knew her well, although, upon reflection, not as well as I thought I did."

"Were you involved with her?"

"If you mean did I sleep with her? Yes, regrettably."

"I'm sorry to hear that." River shifted on the sofa. "I mean, not about the sleeping together part...about the regrettably part."

River reminded herself that this was not a date. She still hoped that Clay might turn out to be a client. But her libido hadn't gotten that message. She'd definitely taken the conversation down a more personal path asking about Veronica, but she'd felt some strange compulsion to know the story behind the photos she'd seen online. A cloud settled over Clay's face, and River was truly sorry. She'd clearly opened some wound for Clay. She got up and retrieved the bottle from the kitchen.

"Veronica Mann is a predator." She poured them both more wine.

"Where were you a year ago with that heads-up?"

River laughed. "Sorry I wasn't there to warn you." River sank back into her corner. "But she's not the reason you left New York is she?"

Clay leaned forward and rubbed her eyes with her free hand. Instinctively, River touched her arm. Clay looked down at River's fingers on her arm and then met River's gaze. Clay was upset, and River felt like a jerk for being so flippant about a subject that Clay hadn't gotten over.

"I should go." Clay stood up.

"Are you sure you can ride after drinking wine?" River had completely ruined the moment, and she wanted a chance to salvage things. And then she remembered. "One of my aunt's neighbors brought over a casserole earlier. I could reheat it if you'll stay."

Clay seemed surprised by the invitation.

"Come on, stay, and no more talk of evil exes, I promise." She was standing close to Clay and couldn't resist touching her arm again. The light contact sent warm tendrils of electric current all through her body. "Besides, I might need help figuring out how to operate the oven."

Clay laughed, and the weight of the air in the room lightened. River couldn't help smiling. She'd managed to bring a smile back to Clay's face and that pleased her.

"I take it the kitchen is not your domain." Clay followed her to the refrigerator.

"Definitely not." River swiveled, setting the large dish on the counter near the oven. "I don't cook. But I have other talents."

"I have no doubt about that."

River was sure she was blushing at the comment and the teasingly flirtatious look that followed. River watched as Clay turned on the stove and set the temperature.

"About this casserole...I'm not exactly sure if this is supposed to be an entrée or dessert."

"In the Deep South, where the words *Jell-O* and *salad* can be used together to describe an entrée, those two things are definitely *not* mutually exclusive."

River laughed. Clay seemed comfortable in her aunt's kitchen, and River was reminded that there was history here for Clay that she knew nothing about. There were things she wanted to ask Clay, but she wasn't sure what safe topics might be.

"I'm surprised I've never met you before. I mean, you know, if you'd visited Eve we'd have probably met sooner." Clay crossed her arms and leaned against the counter as they waited for the oven to reach the proper temperature. River couldn't help noticing Clay's subtly sculpted biceps. Hands and arms. Clay had strong hands and arms, leanly muscled and toned. For an instant, an image flashed through her mind of Clay, hovering above her, braced above her on those arms. River cleared her throat and looked away.

"I wasn't really close to my aunt. You probably already guessed that."

Clay nodded.

"It wasn't by choice. I've only recently discovered that she and my father had a bit of a falling out...um, maybe conflict is more accurate." River didn't really know Clay well enough to go into all the details, and Clay was polite enough not to ask for more.

"That's too bad. Eve was an amazing woman." Clay wandered from the kitchen to the hallway. She examined the photos as she sipped her wine. "I miss her."

"I'm sorry I won't get the chance to know her."

"She's the reason I started painting you know. She helped me get into college too." Clay looked at River.

"Really?" River was curious, but this time she waited for Clay to continue rather than pelting her with questions.

Clay moved slowly down the hallway, pausing to look more closely at particular framed photos as she sipped her wine.

"I remember when this photo was taken." Clay smiled and pointed at one of the images halfway down the hall.

River joined her so that she could have a better look.

"Eve had helped me enter some drawings into a local art competition, and one of the pieces won second place. She and her partner, Peggy, drove me over for the opening in Savannah, and then we all went out for dinner afterward to celebrate."

"Is Peggy...is she..."

"Peggy died several years ago from cancer. She and Eve were together a long time, as long as I can remember anyway." Clay's eyes were heavy lidded and sad. "They lived here together. And I used to stay here sometimes." She pointed toward the doorway opposite the photos several feet away. "That was my room."

"Did something happen with your family?" River was almost afraid to find out. Protectiveness surged at the thought that Clay, at a young age, might have been kicked out of her home for being gay.

"My dad passed away when I was a kid. It was sudden...a heart defect. And my mom married the first man that she dated after." The expression on Clay's face grew more serious as she studied a few other photos along the wall. "He and I never got along, and I think he was more than happy to have Eve mentor me in art so that I was out of his hair and sometimes out from under his roof."

"How old were you when they got married?"

"Thirteen. I was fifteen when he took a job in Tampa and they moved away. There was no way I was gonna go with them. I stayed here with my grandparents. And Eve kept helping me improve my painting skills." The oven chimed and Clay slid the casserole dish onto the middle rack. "It was all for the best. Mom and Gary still live in Tampa. She's happy and I'm happy for her. And I definitely made the right decision to stay here and finish high school with my friends." She leaned against the counter and rested her palms on the edge. "Now you know my whole sad story, including Veronica, and I know hardly anything about you except that you like to drive barefoot, that operating a stove exceeds your technical abilities in the kitchen, and that you own a gallery in the City."

River laughed. "Sorry, have I been asking too many questions?"

"More like I've been talking nonstop." Clay wiggled her empty glass in the air. "I think it's the wine. Maybe I should switch to water if I'm going to ride that bike home."

There was an instant where River almost offered that Clay could stay as long as she liked, but that seemed too forward. Although, as the thought rose and was quickly dismissed, River realized that she liked Clay, really liked her. There was something really solid about Clay. Her presence grounded the air around her, and River had the strongest urge to lean into the weight of it. Not that she wasn't grounded herself, but she was always in motion, and Clay…well, Clay was tranquil, unruffled, and easy. Not just on the eyes. Something about Clay's energy made River relax.

Chapter Thirteen

Clay took one last bite of the casserole and then set her fork down. It was hard not to keep eating, but as it was they'd finished off almost half of it along with one more glass of wine for River. Clay had switched to water because a third glass of Merlot would definitely have impaired her ability to ride home safely.

She still hadn't managed to get too many personal details from River. Maybe she'd been asking the wrong questions.

"Do you run the gallery in New York all by yourself?"

"I have one employee, Amelia. She's a friend from college so she's more of a partner than an assistant."

Did *partner* mean partner or lover?

"How long have you two been together?"

"Oh, when I said partner I didn't mean it like that, I simply meant that we don't have a typical boss, employee relationship. We were friends before we started working together." River pushed her plate aside. They were sitting across from each other, eating on the countertop of the island that separated the kitchen from the living room. "Amelia is great, you'd like her. I told her to google you too. She thought you were really cute, but she's straight, so don't get any ideas." River covered her mouth with her hand. "I can't believe I said that out loud."

The wine was clearly going to her head. She was adorably tipsy.

"I should probably go." Clay stood up. The attraction she was feeling for River hadn't lessened as they'd talked. More wine and conversation was just going to make it harder to leave. Besides, it was getting late. "Thank you for letting me hang out for so long, and for the food. This was really...fun." She realized as soon as she said it that it was true. Tonight had been fun. River was fun. Clay couldn't remember the last time she'd said that about an evening out with anyone. She'd definitely been in a funk for weeks.

"Are you sure you're okay to ride that bike?"

"Oh, yeah, I'm fine. And I don't have that far to go anyway. My place is close by."

River followed her to the door, but didn't open it. They stood facing each other in the low light of the dimly lit living room. A lamp was on across the room, and it highlighted River's profile. She wanted to kiss River. The urge was overwhelming, like she was some small astral body circling a star and gravity was slowly reeling her into a shrinking orbit. She leaned closer, their faces only inches apart. River looked up at her expectantly, her lips slightly parted, but at the last instant before contact, River shifted, kissing her lightly on the cheek. Clay was surprised by the kiss, and she was sure it showed on her face. Was River giving her the brush-off? Friendly and cordial, but a brush-off nonetheless. Clay reached for the door.

"Okay, well, have a good night." Clay wasn't sure what else to say.

"You too." River stood in the doorway as Clay walked to the curb.

Clay tried not to read into what had just happened, but that was almost impossible. What had she expected? She showed up unexpectedly, talked about her ex and her high school drama with her stepfather. What a complete downer she must be. Loads of fun. She was probably lucky River hadn't kicked her to the curb two hours earlier.

Clay smiled thinly at River, who was still standing in the open door, backlit by the living room lamp. She adjusted her helmet and then gave a quick wave before she rode away.

River closed the door and covered her face with her hands. What was that? Clay had most definitely been about to kiss her. There was no doubt about it, and she'd panicked and kissed Clay on the cheek before they could kiss for real. What was wrong with her?

She swept her hands up and then down through her hair. There were a few slices of cheese left on the plate so she put the dish in the fridge and then collected the wineglasses and rinsed them in the sink. There was only a half glass left in the bottle as she held it up to the light, and she knew she'd drunk most of it. Clay had judiciously stopped after her second glass.

She slouched onto the sofa with the wine bottle, staring up at the ceiling fan. She might as well finish the last few sips. River hoisted the bottle to her lips. What a pretty picture this must be? In running shorts and a T-shirt, drinking wine right from the bottle. *Oh, how the mighty have fallen.* She expected to feel more of a buzz, but the almost kiss seemed to have chased the alcohol right out of her bloodstream. Thoughts circulated in her annoyingly clear head. She'd derailed the kiss because she knew deep down that she was interested in Clay. She was attracted to Clay.

During her call with Amelia, she'd said she was going to linger in Pine Cone to convince Clay into letting her gallery represent Clay's work. That wasn't going to work now. River knew without a doubt that she had genuine feelings for Clay. After what she now knew about Veronica, there was no way she'd cross that line by sleeping with an artist she hoped to represent. That had always been her professional policy anyway, but now it seemed even more important to keep that boundary clear.

There was no doubt in her mind that she wanted to kiss Clay Cahill. After spending a few hours with Clay, her body ached for much more than a kiss. She'd panicked in that moment of potential intimacy as they said good-bye, but the path seemed obvious to her now. Somewhere between smoked Gouda and pineapple casserole, River had made the clear decision that she wanted Clay in her bed, not on her gallery walls.

She smiled as she launched herself up from the cozy sofa and shuffled, bottle in hand, to the room where Clay had slept. That was definitely where she was going to spend the night. Visualizing a certain dark-haired dream date riding a sleek black Italian motorcycle.

Chapter Fourteen

River gradually fought her way out of sleep. Her head was pounding. No, wait, there was actual pounding coming from somewhere outside. River squinted as she tugged the drapes aside. Natalie Payne was standing on the front lawn watching some burly guy hammer a For Sale sign into the ground. Natalie nodded and waved him off as he gathered posthole diggers and a large mallet and stowed them in his truck. Natalie turned toward the house as if she were about to head for the front door.

River sat up too quickly. Okay, now her head was pounding too. She swiveled and let her toes touch the cool hardwood floor for a second while her swimming head settled. The empty wine bottle mocked her from the nightstand. By the time she reached the living room, still in her shorts and T-shirt from the night before, Natalie was knocking on the door.

"Well, someone had fun last night." Natalie's mood was as intense as the early morning sun and just as unwelcome.

"Hi, Natalie."

"Here, I brought these by. I'll leave them in the box out front that's mounted on the sign post, but I wanted you to have one." She turned and waved toward the pristine white post holding the real estate company's logo along with Natalie's name and number. "I wanted to make sure you saw the sign. We're in business."

"Thank you."

"I see you still have Clay's truck. And I couldn't help noticing that sexy bike of hers parked out front last night when Ted and I drove home from dinner out." Natalie quirked one side of her mouth up as she teased River.

"Yes, she stopped by to give me some information about my aunt's car."

"I'll bet she did." Natalie patted her arm cheerfully. "Well, I'm off. You let me know if you need anything. And don't forget about the downtown market tonight. You'll want to check that out for sure. I'll call you to set up viewing times once we start getting calls. You watch, we'll sell this place in no time." She waved at River as she started across the lawn toward her car. "Toodles!"

Toodles? What sort of person said toodles? River scowled and shook her head as she closed the door, giving herself a respite from the blazing sun. She was *not* a morning person, even without alcohol consumption. As her brain began to wake up, so did her stomach. Her purchases from the previous night weren't exactly breakfast fare. River decided to shower and then go in search of food. Surely she could get something either at the bakery she'd passed on her first drive through town or at the Dogwood Diner.

There was a bit of a line at Hot Buns Bakery. Chatter from an array of patrons created a low buzz inside the cozy breakfast spot. As might be expected, there were people eating and talking, and then there were others who looked as if they'd set up a small satellite office for the day, laptops and cell phones and random papers strewn about their tables.

"What can I get for you, hon?" The most adorable gay guy with a thick Southern drawl rested his hands on the counter and smiled at River.

This was the gayest small town she'd ever been in. She was distracted for an instant wondering, not for the first time, if something was in the water in Pine Cone. It must be great to feel part of a settled, rural community and still be able to be completely who you were.

"Um, can I get a latte?"

"Yes, you may. For here?"

She nodded and he passed a cup to a barista at the espresso machine behind him. The barista was probably in her early twenties, with long dark hair pulled back into a very loose knot. Her arms were covered with full sleeves of tattoos. The pattern was mesmerizing.

"Anything else?" His voice brought her attention back to the register.

"Oh, sorry, yes, can I have one of those breakfast croissants?"

"Egg and cheese?"

"Yes, please."

"Would you like me to warm it up for you?"

"That would be great, thank you."

"Can I get a name for your order? I'll bring it out to you when it's ready."

"River."

"Hi, River, I'm Preston. Nice to meet you." He extended his hand across the counter and she shook it.

"Nice to meet you, Preston." This was a lot of friendliness before coffee, but River was trying her best to keep up. It wasn't that she was grouchy in the morning, it was simply that she wasn't quite awake first thing. She never really felt awake until after her second cup of coffee and preferred to keep human interaction at a minimum until that second cup threshold had been reached.

River found a small table near the window that had just been vacated and took a seat. She looked out the window and plotted her day. There were more things to go through at the gallery. She needed to decide whether to ship any of the pieces to New York. She'd forgotten to ask Clay about the three paintings. Would she want them back? Might she want River to sell them for her? She doubted it, but maybe she was wrong about that.

River scrolled through messages on her phone, looking up briefly when her latte and croissant were delivered to her table by Preston.

❖

Clay had overslept so she hadn't had time to make coffee before getting to the shop to open up. She only managed to beat Eddie by a couple of minutes. Bo was late as usual. After one cup of her grandpa's brand of gas station coffee, she decided to make a drink run to Hot Buns.

"Do you want anything?" She jangled her keys.

"Nah, I'm good."

Eddie had lower standards for his morning brew than Clay. Urban coffee shops had ruined her. Luckily, her friend Preston had an espresso machine, and he was only minutes away. She debated taking the tow truck so she could get the coffee to go, but it was big and hard to park anywhere along Main Street. She'd just ride her bike and drink it there. Today seemed like a slow day at the garage anyway.

The morning rush had died down and there was no one in line when she arrived, although the place was at capacity. A low-level hum of conversation and the hiss of steam from the frother greeted her as she approached the front counter to order.

"Hi, Preston, can I get a latte?"

"Hi, sweetie. For here or to go?"

Preston Howard III made gay look good. He was tall and fit with killer good looks. He had light brown hair with perfect blond sun-bleached streaks and a perpetual tan. He was also a great wingman when her bestie, Trip, wasn't available, and Clay was in the mood to hit the clubs in Savannah. But that hadn't happened in a long time. Not since before she moved to New York City and then moved back, under a cloud of failure.

"I'm on the bike, so not exactly hands-free this morning." She fished in her pocket for cash. "I'll just drink it here."

Preston gave the barista her order, then leaned conspiratorially across the counter toward her. "Hottie, two o'clock." He made the slightest motion of his head toward the front corner of the bakery.

"What? Where?" She followed his gaze to see River, head down, taking a sip of her coffee in between bursts of typing on her phone.

"Am I right or am I right?"

"You're not wrong." Clay hadn't seen River until Preston pointed her out, and River still hadn't seen her. "She's beautiful." She spoke quietly enough that only Preston would have been able to hear it, and only if he'd been listening intently.

"Then why are you still standing here?"

"You're making me a latte, remember?"

"And then what?"

"I'm thinking."

Preston shook his head and smiled. "No guts no glory," he muttered under his breath.

"That line only really works in war movies, you know." She crossed her arms and waited for her coffee. Maybe Preston was right; it did take a certain amount of emotional fortitude to put yourself out there. She needed to man up. Or not.

"Still driving that truck?" He tweaked an eyebrow as he passed a cup, along with her order, to the cute barista nearby.

"It's a living."

"I'm just waiting for the morning when you stroll up and tell me this is your last latte from Hot Buns because you're moving back to New York to be a star." He reached in the case and handed her a cookie on the house while she waited for her coffee. "I'm living vicariously through you, ya know."

Clay took a bite. "Ha." A few powder-fine cookie crumbs escaped. "As if."

She tried to stay focused on Preston, but River kept infiltrating her peripheral vision.

"I'm serious." Preston made a big show of wiping the counter down with a cloth. "How am I going to find a hot boyfriend in the Big Apple if you're not there to take me out on the town?"

"You know you can visit New York even if I'm not living there?"

"Not the same."

She considered taking the coffee to go. The brush-off she'd gotten from River the previous night still puzzled her. More than that, it agitated her. She'd finally given in to her attraction, and when she'd attempted to make the first move, River shot her down with a sisterly kiss on the cheek. What was that about?

Should she take a hint and leave before River saw her?

Too late.

Just in that instant, River glanced up and casually scanned the café as she sipped her coffee. Her gaze froze on Clay, pinning her to the counter where she waited for her latte. She swallowed the last of the cookie and tried to act cool. Clay averted her eyes, but when she looked back, River was still watching her and gave a little wave as if she wasn't sure Clay had seen her. Clay waved back.

"I think that was an invitation." Preston handed her a large steaming cup with a little heart shape in the frothed milk.

"Nice touch."

Clay took her time getting to River's table. She was taking a moment to try, through force of will, not to care, but it was impossible. She did care.

River stood up as she approached.

"Good morning, I'm so happy to run into you."

"Hi."

"Will you join me?"

River clicked her phone off, flipped it face down, and then motioned to the empty chair across from hers.

"I just have a few minutes, then I have to get back to the shop."

They both sat down.

"That's okay, I'm not staying long either. I have to get back to some work on my laptop. New York doesn't shut down while I'm away." River rested her elbows on the table and leaned forward a little. Her eyes were bright. She'd pulled her hair back and was wearing a snug fitting cotton blouse, jeans, and sandals. Somehow River managed to look casual and elegant at the same time.

"My grandpa's coffee is terrible. I decided I had to have a little shot of espresso to jump-start this day."

"Is it my fault?"

Clay considered how best to answer that question. Replaying the good night kiss scene in an endless loop inside her head for hours had certainly kept Clay up late. So the short answer was yes, it was River's fault, but she didn't particularly feel like owning up to that.

"Why would it be your fault?"

"Oh, you know, because of the wine." River tucked a loose wisp of hair behind her ear. "I managed to finish the bottle after you left. Possibly not the wisest choice."

"Really?"

"Oh, good, now you think I'm a lush."

The self-effacing comment helped Clay relax a little.

"It was good wine."

"And I'm sure I impressed you with my culinary prowess." River studied Clay over the rim of her coffee mug.

Was River flirting? If she was, Clay wasn't falling into it this time, like she had with Veronica. She was fairly certain, given the chaste kiss from the previous night, that River was simply flirtatious by nature and didn't mean anything by it. Clay bit her lower lip and glanced out the window. Unfortunately, she wasn't immune to River's charms, whether she meant it or not. Butterflies had set up shop in her stomach. This was not the relaxed coffee break she'd imagined.

"Listen, about last night—"

"There you are." Grace cut River off as she swept through the door.

"Oh, hey." Clay looked up, coffee in hand.

"I need you out on Highway 58, near our cutoff to the river." Grace was all business but seemed to finally register that River was seated at the table with Clay. "Sorry to interrupt your coffee date. Hi, River."

"It's not a—"

"It's nice to see you, Grace." River cut Clay off this time. She turned to Clay, a look of frustration on her face.

Why was River frustrated? From Clay's standpoint, she'd been holding all the cards so far, in whatever this was, which was certainly not a date.

"I called the shop and Eddie told me you were here. I called your cell, but apparently you don't have it on you."

Instinctively, Clay ran her hand over the pockets of her jeans. She must have set it down somewhere absently. She'd been more than a little distracted this morning.

"I'll drive back now, get the truck, and meet you there. What happened?" Clay took a big gulp of her latte.

"Lynette blew a tire and went off the road. I've got a call in to the rescue squad. We need their help too, but we can't even get to the car until we can winch it out. It's wedged tightly between two trees…Lynette has her sister's baby in the car with her. Jamie is on the scene already. She got the call first."

"I'm on my way." Clay stood and downed the rest of her coffee. It was still early, but the inside of a car got hot quickly in South Georgia. Worry chased the butterflies away as she jumped into action.

"Be careful." River stood too. Grace was out the door already.

"Thanks." Clay was out the door quickly, cranked her bike and followed Grace's squad car, lights flashing, siren blaring. If only she'd driven the truck in the first place she'd have been able to respond sooner.

CHAPTER FIFTEEN

Clay could see the rear bumper of Lynette's car angled up at an unnatural slant just past the shoulder of the road. Two squad cars were parked along the lane where the car had crossed and gone off the highway and an ambulance was nearby. Two members of the rescue squad hovered beside the old Chevy talking to Lynette through a partially broken window. Flares warned any approaching traffic to slow and go around the site. Jamie was on traffic duty, standing farthest away from the errant Chevy.

"See how it's wedged between those two trees?" Grace pointed as Clay walked up. The car was perfectly centered, jammed between two pine trees. "The doors are completely blocked on both sides. Rescue squad can't get in there until we pull the car out."

"Got it. Let me just tell Lynette what's happening." She didn't want Lynette to be scared when the car started to move. As she got near the broken window, she could hear the faint whimper of Lynette's two-year-old niece, Ashley. "Hey, Lynette, I'm gonna pull the car back with the winch."

"Clay! Am I glad to see you." Even in the dimly lit auto's interior, Clay could see the uneasiness on Lynette's face.

"Hang on just a minute more, we'll get you outta there."
Clay nodded to the two guys from the rescue squad and they
stepped back to give her room.

Once the chains were attached to the frame of the car's
undercarriage, Clay ran the winch until the chain was taut and
she heard the sound of metal creaking and scraping. The winch
wined loudly. She'd use the winch just to get the car past the trees
enough for the guys to free Lynette and Ashley, then she'd use the
full power of the tow truck to pull the car the rest of the way up
and onto the pavement. The last part would get a bit rough so she
wanted Lynette and Ashley out of harm's way for that.

"It's clear!" one of the guys yelled. He was watching the
progress from a vantage point closer to where the car was stuck.

Clay halted the winch until she got the signal that Lynette
and Ashley were free. Grace was standing at a halfway point
between the driver's side door and where Clay was. After what
seemed like a long two minutes, she waved to Clay.

"They're all clear." Grace made a circular motion with her
hand to signal that Clay could continue.

She got the car up to an almost level angle. Clay unhooked
the winch line so that she could change the angle of the truck
and load the car properly onto the tow gear. Huge gash marks
streaked both sides of the car. It was something of a miracle that
Lynette had managed to miss hitting one of the trees head-on
and instead had gone right between them.

With the car hoisted up at an angle, she could see Ashley's
pink car seat peeking up from the backseat, and her stomach
clenched. This accident could have been a whole lot worse.

Grace left Lynette and Ashley with the rescue squad and
walked toward Clay. Lynette was sipping from a paper cup
while seated at the open back door of the ambulance. Jamie
hovered nearby, holding the leash of a fluffy, medium-sized dog

that looked like Toto's cousin, only about twice the size. Ashley was kneeling next to the dog, hugging its neck.

"Is Lynette okay?"

"Just shaken up." Grace braced her hands on her utility belt and surveyed Lynette's car. "Thank goodness she was in a pocket of cell service here, otherwise it might have taken a lot longer for someone to spot the car."

"Who's dog?"

"That's Petunia, the newest member of our law enforcement team."

"No kidding?"

"She's a drug-sniffing dog."

"Right now she's doing an amazing impersonation of a teddy bear." Clay tipped her head in Ashley's direction, her arms wrapped around Petunia.

"Emergencies call for all sorts of first responders." Grace smiled.

"Should I wait?"

"No, you can take off. We're almost finished with the accident report, and then I'll drive Lynette to her sister's house."

Clay reached for the door to climb in.

"Oh, and sorry I ruined your breakfast date with River." Grace smirked over her shoulder as she strode back toward the accident scene.

Clay scowled after Grace. Why did everyone keep calling it a date?

She planted one boot on the runner board and launched herself into the truck. This truck started life as a one-ton dual axle pickup truck. But then her grandpa added a state-of-the-art hydraulics package, steel plating, and a large capacity hoisting arm. This truck demanded respect on the road, and on frequent occasions awarded Clay hero status.

In a driver's hour of need, she came to the rescue. Being someone's hero, being anyone's hero, was pretty damn fulfilling while she figured out what to do with the rest of her life.

❖

The downtown market was well underway by the time River parked about a block off Main Street. It was around five thirty, maybe closer to six, and she hadn't really had a proper lunch so the smell of grilled edibles from several nearby food vendors made her stomach growl.

She'd attempted to get some work done on her gallery's quarterly taxes but had been interrupted twice by calls from Natalie wanting to show the house to prospective buyers. Since she was anxious to get things moving and return to New York, there was no other option than to accommodate the tours through her aunt's house.

It wasn't as if she'd been close to her aunt, but even still, having strangers walk through and comment on items in the house felt invasive. River found herself feeling protective of a woman she'd never really known. Maybe it was Clay's connection to her aunt that made her feel some kinship.

Clay had lurked around the edges of her mind all day. Running into Clay at the bakery that morning would have been, could have been, the perfect chance to clear the air a bit, but then Grace had shown up with some emergency and Clay left so quickly that River didn't get to explain. What would she have said anyway? Sorry, I meant to kiss you for real but I missed?

This was one of those instances when actions would speak louder than words. She needed to see Clay and simply show her how she felt. How did she feel? Maybe she should sort out the answer to that question first.

Attraction? Check.

Intellectual connection? Check.

Available? Hmm, unknown.

Yes, Clay was single, but was she truly emotionally available? River wasn't quite sure. Clay was willing to make the first move last night so at least that meant she was open to some sort of physical connection, probably. River wasn't going to be in town that much longer anyway, so did it really matter if Clay was emotionally available or not? It wasn't as if River was looking for some serious thing with someone who lived eight hundred miles away from New York.

"Hey, River!"

She'd been lost in thought when someone called her name. She scanned the crowd for a few seconds before she saw Trip waving her over to a cluster of tables surrounded by folding chairs. River smiled and waved.

"Hi, Trip."

"I'm happy to see you're checking out our local culture." Trip stood near her half-eaten plate of food, and offered River a chair.

"My Realtor suggested I investigate the downtown market. Something smells good." River surveyed the food vendors nearby.

"I recommend the barbecue from Willis's truck right there." Trip pointed toward a bright red food truck several yards away.

"Okay, I'll take your advice."

"Wait, you sit. Let me buy you dinner."

"No, really—"

"I insist. Please, sit…I'll get something for you."

Trip was definitely chivalrous; River would have to give her points for that. She nodded. "Okay, if you insist."

"I insist. You can't go back to New York until you've tasted Willis's pulled pork."

A few moments later, Trip returned with a heaping plate that included slaw, hush puppies, and pickles on the side. There was no way she'd be able to eat such a heaping portion, but she accepted the plate gratefully and dug in. Trip was right; the meat was succulent and delicious. Several people stopped by to speak with Trip as they ate. It was obvious that she was well liked in this community.

"You're so popular," River teased her.

"Well, the residents of Pine Cone love their show horses and livestock. And I love taking good care of their animals. So, it's sort of like we're family, connected through a myriad of four-legged friends."

"I'm not convinced it's simply about the animal care. I think you have a fan club, Dr. Beaumont."

"Thank you. You're sweet to say that." Trip smiled. "Hey, listen, I'm having a cookout at my house tomorrow. You should come."

"Oh, I don't know—"

"Absolutely, I won't take no for an answer. It'll just be a lot of locals. Clay will be there...and Grace...you'll know a few people for sure. You should come."

"Really?" River wasn't so sure.

"Yes, really." She handed River her phone. "Put your number in there, and I'll text you the address so you'll have it."

"Shall I bring something?"

"Just yourself...it's open bar with lots of craft beer and mixed drinks. The wine will be pretty stock, so you might want to bring your own if you're a connoisseur." Trip folded her hands on the table as River entered her phone number.

River wondered if the invitation was simply a ploy to get her phone number, but Trip's invitation seemed more friendly than flirtatious. And the chance to see Clay in a relaxed social setting was appealing enough to be worth the risk. Plus, she'd completely forgotten to ask Clay about keeping the truck a little longer. It wasn't her fault, Clay was more than a little distracting.

"I usually crank the grill up around four o'clock. Come any time after that."

"Thanks for the invitation."

Music had started to drift in their direction from the gazebo in the center of the main square. A band was playing covers of classic seventies music, and quite a few couples had drifted to the gazebo to dance.

"Do you like to dance?"

"Sure, I love to dance."

"Want to?"

The question caught River off guard. "Dance? Now?"

"I mean, unless you're going to eat the plate too."

River looked down and laughed, realizing she'd eaten every bite of the heaped BBQ. Maybe she should dance before she ended up licking the plate clean.

"Yes, I think I'm finished. I'd love to dance."

Trip held out her arm and they wound through onlookers until they found an open space. River wondered if anyone would take issue with two women dancing together, but no one seemed to pay them any attention. She relaxed and allowed herself to enjoy the music. The tune the band was playing reminded her of a seventies-themed party her sorority had hosted when she was in college. The memory made her smile.

Chapter Sixteen

Clay forgot it was Wednesday and realized too late that Main Street was blocked off for the market all around the central downtown square. Well, she might as well park the bike and get some food. She probably had something at her place if she was in the mood to eat breakfast for dinner, but scrambled eggs didn't sound appealing and she didn't really feel like cooking.

She spotted Grace managing crowd control. Grace had a real gift for appearing nonchalant while at the same time commanding respect. It was one of the things Clay liked about Grace. She was as sweet as she could be, but you didn't disrespect her authority or your ass would be in a sling for sure.

"How's it going?" Clay sauntered up just as Grace signaled for a teenage boy to get off his skateboard.

"Good. The usual. Just keeping an eye on rowdy teenagers and free-range children." Grace stepped a few feet away. "I said, get that skateboard off the sidewalk, and I don't mean later, I mean right now."

"Yes, ma'am." He picked up his board and shuffled off with his friends.

"Don't ma'am me," Grace muttered. "I really hate being called ma'am. Do I look that old?"

"I don't think it's an age thing, I think it's the firearm and the uniform."

"Well, it sounds old." Grace crossed her arms and stood scanning the slowly milling crowd. "What are you up to?"

"I was going home but thought I'd pick up food first."

"Good call. I had something earlier."

"Okay, well, I'll catch you later." Clay started walking toward a cluster of food trucks on the next block.

"Hey, are you going to Trip's cookout tomorrow?"

"I was planning on it."

"Okay then, I'll see you there. You should invite River."

"Maybe."

Grace shook her head.

Clay hadn't really talked to Grace or Trip since she'd spent the evening with River and gotten the brush-off. Rescuing Lynette from her banged up Chevy was more important than deciphering a kiss on the cheek. Besides, once she opened that door she'd never hear the end of it from Grace. In all likelihood she would *not* be inviting River.

Clay opted for a chicken teriyaki bowl so that she could easily walk around the art and craft booths while she ate. She'd slowly ambled down an entire block of white tent covered booths and was almost at the edge of the square when she saw them.

River and Trip, dancing.

She froze like a deer who'd just heard a rifle shot, food half chewed and packed into her cheek like a chipmunk, fork midair.

River was laughing and dancing with Clay's best friend.

This was one of those moments when rational thought might have informed Clay that this situation was harmless. That Trip had no designs on River and that they were simply having a friendly dance. But rational thought had vacated the premises.

Rational thought had left the building for a beer run, leaving irrational thought alone in the house to make bad choices.

Jealousy flamed out of nowhere catching Clay by surprise. She swallowed the food she no longer had a taste for just as Trip turned her way.

Clay looked away charting her escape, but Trip waved her over. It was too late now anyway, because River had seen her too.

"Hey, man, your timing is perfect. I need you to cut in so I can give my bum knee a rest." Trip patted Clay on the shoulder.

That was a tall tale. Trip was in top shape, probably better than Clay even, but every time she wanted to talk Clay into doing something, she'd blame an old college basketball injury that seemed to flare up conveniently.

Clay didn't respond. She just stood there staring mutely between River and Trip.

"Here, I'll finish that for you so your hands are free." Trip took the almost empty bowl of rice and chicken out of Clay's hand and good-naturedly shoved her toward the spot where she'd been standing next to River.

"We can take a break." River seemed to be offering Clay an out.

Clay's mouth was open, the words were on the tip of her tongue, but Trip jumped in.

"No way. Clay loves to dance." Trip wacked her on the back. "Right?"

Clay frowned at her.

"I'll just go sit over here and rest my knee." Trip pointed toward a chair. She smiled at Clay. They'd been best friends forever so Clay knew good and well that Trip understood every nuance of her nonverbal communication and was choosing to ignore them all. Especially when River was around. She watched Trip fake limp to a folding chair.

Clay wasn't sure dancing with River was a good idea, but now she was stuck. Very pleasantly stuck, but stuck nonetheless. As luck would have it, the moment she turned to face River, the band transitioned to a slow song. Clay tried to get her heart to settle; it was thumping so loud that she was certain River would be able to hear it above the music.

River casually stepped closer, taking Clay's hand and draping her arm around Clay's shoulder. That did it. Nerve receptors hummed, shifted into overdrive, and the tingling sensation rippled through Clay's entire body. River looked up, and those eyes…those eyes vaulted past all her defenses. She had trouble remembering what she was defending in the first place. As the vanilla scent of River's skin invaded her senses, she wanted nothing more than to tear down all the walls and let her in.

River sensed it the instant Clay relaxed. She'd initially taken River's hand stiffly, and just now she loosened her grip. Noticing the change, River glanced up. There was something different in the way Clay looked at her too. Molten warmth spread through her chest and eased down to her core. This was all she'd hoped for all day. A chance to be close to Clay and make things right.

There was hardly any space between their bodies, but hers reacted to Clay's nearness. Every subtle brush of contact as they swayed to the music echoed in her chest, her heart ratcheting up a little with each touch. She closed her eyes allowing the sensations to wash over her.

"Clay!"

River was startled by the sound of a woman's voice. Clay seemed to know her. She took a step back and dropped River's hand just as the woman captured Clay in a hug. River moved away to avoid an elbow. The exuberant woman seemed oblivious to her presence.

"Thank you, thank you! Clay, you saved my life today." The woman looked like Jessica Simpson's version of Daisy Duke, and she was practically climbing Clay's long frame.

"Lynette, I'm just glad you're okay." Clay tried to gently pry Lynette's arms from around her neck. She gave River a sideways look as if she wanted to apologize for the abrupt interruption. "Lynette, this is River."

"Do you know this woman saved my life today?" Lynette looked briefly at River but refused to release Clay and instead held Clay's face in her hands and kissed her. It was a quick kiss on the lips, like a reward or something, but it still didn't sit well with River and she wasn't sure exactly what to do about it. It was clear that this woman knew Clay, probably too well.

"Uh, no, I didn't know." River tried her best not to sound annoyed.

"Well, she did."

"Lynette, it wasn't that big of a deal." This time Clay succeeded in separating herself from Lynette's effusive display. "Lynette's car went off the road this morning. That was why Grace stopped by the bakery to get me."

At least part of the picture started to make sense to River.

"It *was* a big deal, and I plan to make it up to you. You just name the date." Lynette flirtatiously twirled a lock of her hair with one manicured finger and touched the center of Clay's chest with another. Clay didn't respond as Lynette turned to go. She looked back, smiling. "Nice to meet you, River."

Whatever had been happening during their first dance had gotten completely derailed by a tornado of hair, cleavage, and barely-there cutoff shorts. River looked down and couldn't help feeling as if her tasteful sleeveless top and linen shorts had been completely overwhelmed by Lynette's tsunami of boobs and hair. She sighed as Lynette was swallowed up by the crowd.

"Let's get out of here."

"What?" The pace of the next song had picked up along with the volume. River wasn't sure she'd heard what Clay said.

"Do you want to get out of here?" Clay's focus was intense. Her gaze created a thread of current that rippled through River's stomach.

"Yes, I'd like that very much."

Clay took her hand as they wound toward the crowd.

"Where'd you park?"

"Oh, um, down there, past the burrito truck. About a block away." River realized she still had Clay's truck, and because of that, Clay was relegated to two-wheeled transportation. She wouldn't have said no to a spin on Clay's bike, but it seemed Clay wasn't offering that up.

They reached the truck and Clay held out her hand for the key. Clay opened the driver's side door and waited for River to slide in. River stayed close, in the middle of the bench seat, as Clay turned the truck around and headed toward the sunset.

"Did you really save Lynette's life today?" River couldn't help wondering what else Clay may have done for Lynette.

"That was a bit of an exaggeration."

"Not from her perspective."

Clay looked over and smiled, but didn't respond.

"Where are we going?"

"I thought it'd be nice to drive out a ways and watch the sunset." Clay slowed and made a right turn just at the edge of town. "I just wanted to pick up something at my place first."

River watched from the truck as Clay opened the door to what looked like a warehouse and disappeared inside. A minute later, she came back with a small leather bag. She slid it behind the seat before she got in.

"That's very mysterious." River joked.

"Not really, but I think you'll like it."

Now River was really intrigued, but patiently waited for this little mystery to reveal itself.

"Is that where you live?"

"Yeah, it used to be a peach packing warehouse."

River was dying to see what the inside looked like. She imagined canvases and paints and sketches strewn about. The thought of it gave her chills. She was completely taken with the artistic process. She loved to see behind the scenes, the sketches, the color studies, reference materials, all of it. She was a process junkie. But she'd have to save that exploration for another time.

They drove for about fifteen minutes, taking two side roads off the highway, before Clay pulled off next to an old wooden one-lane bridge. The timbers were dark with creosote and age. The structure looked like one of the train crossings she'd seen in old movies. But there were no train tracks in view. River climbed out as Clay backed the truck up so that the cab faced away from the sinking sun. River stood at the footing of the bridge watching the wide, slow waterway. Bullfrogs sounded off in the distance, signaling the day's end. She turned around when she heard Clay lower the truck's creaky tailgate.

River eyed the distance from the ground to the tailgate.

"Want some help?"

River nodded. Clay put her hands at River's waist and helped her hop backward up onto the gate, then Clay joined her. Her jean-clad thigh brushed River's leg as they sat side-by-side. Clay had a small flask in her hand. She took a sip and offered it to River.

"Where did that come from?"

"I picked it up at the house." Clay gave River a slow, heart-stopping smile. "It's for emergencies."

"Those seem to happen a lot around here." River accepted the small silver flask and took a tiny sip. The whiskey was warm in her throat. She took a second swig hoping it would help unwind the nerves bundled in her stomach.

The sun sank further, now only a half visible red-orange orb. Color flamed across the smooth surface of the glassy water as if loosely painted with a dry brush.

"This is the Altamaha." Clay seemed to sense her question before she asked it.

"It's so…peaceful."

"I love this river." Clay seemed lost in thought. "This is what I missed the most when I was in New York."

"I've been thinking about you and New York."

"Have you?" Clay handed her the flask again.

"Yes." River took a sip. "Don't let anyone take New York away from you."

"Easy for you to say."

"I know that Veronica is attractive, magnetic, persuasive, and that she uses people and then discards them. Whatever happened between you two, it wasn't your fault."

"I was naïve…and stupid."

She could hear the recrimination in Clay's voice. The last desperate light of the day reflected in her dark eyes. But Clay didn't seem angry, the way she had at the diner when they'd first spoken about her painting. She looked relaxed, thoughtful. It was a good look.

"We're all stupid sometimes." River accepted the flask again. As her fingers brushed against Clay's, she had the urge to reach for her, to entwine their fingers. Like a schoolgirl, she wanted so much just to hold Clay's hand.

"I guess I was her type."

"Success is Veronica's type."

That made Clay smile.

"You think my paintings are good?" Clay asked as if she really didn't know.

"Yes, Clay, they're very good."

Clay hopped down and walked around to the cab of the truck. In this twilight hour, the dome light of the truck shined brightly, casting River's shadow long and away until it was swallowed up by the dark. She wasn't sure what Clay was doing until she heard music. Clay closed the door and darkness consumed them again; there remained only the faintest feather of light along the horizon where the sun had been lost.

River recognized the song. It was a classic, one of her favorites. She hopped down coming face-to-face with Clay just as Elvis began to croon, "Can't Help Falling In Love."

Clay took River's hand and spun her around, softly singing the next line along with the song. "There's nothing like a little Elvis to round out the day."

In her head, River tried not to read into the lyrics, but the words still washed over her in a way she hadn't expected. She shivered and Clay pulled her close.

"You know what I think?" Clay's lips were so close, her words as soft as a caress.

"What do you think?"

"I think you're a country girl trapped in a city girl's body."

"Oh, you do, huh?"

"Yeah." Clay's hand was at the small of her back, keeping as little space between them as possible.

"What gave me away?" River draped her arms around Clay's neck, closed her eyes, and brushed her forehead against Clay's lips. The deepening darkness made her want to feel Clay against her skin.

"Your complete disdain for shoes and—"

She covered Clay's mouth with hers, swallowing the words. River was finished with words for the moment. She wanted to taste Clay. River wanted Clay to feel what she'd been unable or unwilling to say.

Clay gave in to the kiss, she relaxed into it, drawing River close. The soft crush of River against her chest, her lips, her tongue. Clay swept her hand up the curve of River's spine to the base of her neck as the kiss deepened. She felt River's fingers in the short hair at the back of her head as she slid her other hand into Clay's back pocket and squeezed.

The kiss subsided, but they continued to gently sway to the music. River leaned against Clay's shoulder.

"Do you think the song is true?"

"What do you mean?"

"That it's foolish to rush in."

"Let's find out." Clay whispered. "Kiss me again."

River smiled and pulled Clay down until their lips met, tenderly possessive, full of want and wishes. They slow-danced in the moonlight beside the lazy waterway; cicadas and tree frogs joined the melody offering their own summertime chorus.

Chapter Seventeen

Friday came and went almost as a daydream for River. She'd tried to sort things out in the gallery, to make some plan for what to do with all the remaining inventory, but she was so easily distracted. With each distraction, she was more anxious for time to pass so she could see Clay again. Clay had invited her out for dinner, but River didn't know where they were going, only the time.

Her phone rang. Another distraction. This was hopeless. She crossed the gallery and reached for her phone.

"Hey, how's your day going?" The soft cadence of Clay's smooth drawl rippled through River's stomach. River was fairly sure everything sounded sexier with a Southern accent.

"Slow." River perched on the edge of the desk and absently twirled a paper clip.

"Well, I just called to tell you to wear jeans tonight."

"You don't like skirts?" River couldn't help the flirtation.

"I love skirts." Clay faltered. "I mean, not for myself, I wouldn't wear one…but I love skirts on you."

Her comment had caused satisfactory flustering on the other end of the line.

"Okay, but why am I wearing jeans?"

"Because it's hard to ride a motorcycle in a skirt."

"I see your point." River thrilled at the thought of riding the bike with Clay. She was nervous and excited all at the same time.

"I'll pick you up at six." Clay paused. "And, River?"

"Yes."

"Wear sensible shoes."

"I'm not sure what that even means, but I'll try." River clicked off, smiling.

Not really knowing how to anticipate what she'd need for the trip to Georgia, River had packed a little of everything in her giant rolling bag. Since she'd already stayed longer than she'd planned, this had turned out to be a good decision. For tonight's ride she'd chosen a camisole under a sheer top in an attempt to dress up the jeans a little. She checked the full-length mirror one more time after she applied lipstick, deciding she liked the contrast of elegant and casual together. Now for shoes. What did sensible shoes look like other than running shoes, which she was absolutely *not* wearing on a date. She dug in her bag and pulled out a pair of pumps with a short, wide heel. That was as sensible as she was prepared to be.

About three minutes before six o'clock, River heard the distinct sound of a motorcycle. She pulled the drapes aside to check. Clay dismounted, but River dashed out the door before Clay made it all the way up the walkway.

Clay was dressed in a black dress shirt, dark jeans, and black boots with a buckle across the ankle. It was the first time she'd seen Clay in anything other than a T-shirt and work boots. She looked good, very good. She'd obviously also tried to tame her short hair with product. It mostly worked, however, the longer hair in front had broken free of the hold and fallen across one eyebrow in a sexy haphazard way.

Clay handed River a helmet as she walked up.

"You look great." River accepted the shiny black head gear that had double white racing stripes across the curved surface.

"So do you." Clay smiled broadly. "For the record, you look really good in jeans."

"Thank you." River cinched the chinstrap. "Now, where is it you're taking me on this beast?"

Clay swung her leg over the bike and braced it with both feet flat on the ground so River could sit behind her. River had decided she wanted Clay between her legs, but she hadn't expected this would be the way it would happen. The slant of the seat caused her to slide forward. She was flush against Clay's back with her thighs touching Clay's hips.

"We're going to a place about twenty minutes away, toward Savannah. You'll like it." Clay turned partway so River could hear her. "It's called Howard Station. It's an old roadhouse that's now a restaurant. Preston's parents own it."

River remembered Preston from the bakery.

"Hold on." Clay cranked the bike, and they were off.

River tightened her arms around Clay's waist and leaned into her. She was careful to mimic the angle of Clay's body when they turned so their bodies became one unit, moving in unison, working to offset the torque and angle of the bike.

It was the quickest twenty minutes of her life and incredibly exhilarating. River decided it would be very easy to fall in love with a motorcycle. Especially if Clay Cahill came with the bike.

River whipped her hair back and ran her fingers through it after removing the helmet. After a few seconds, she realized Clay was watching her intently.

"What?" River stilled and looked at Clay.

Clay cleared her throat and shook her head. "Nothing." As they walked up the front steps of the restaurant Clay reached to open the restaurant's door for River. "It's just that I think I could stand around and watch you take that helmet off all day."

River stepped past her, smiling.

Howard Station was packed. Almost every table was full. Between the aged pine, tongue and groove paneling, hardwood floors, and the rough-hewn board and beam ceiling, there was very little to absorb the sound of all the chatter inside the restaurant.

"I called ahead and asked for a table on the back porch. It'll be quieter out there." Clay stood near the podium waiting for the hostess to return from seating a party of four near the large stone fireplace.

The hearth wasn't lit, of course, it was too warm, but the smell of a wood fire lingered from past fires. River could image this was a very cozy spot to be when the weather cooled.

The back porch was open and airy, the tables adorned with blue Mason jars filled with fresh cut wildflowers. The porch had a high ceiling where equally spaced fans spun lazily. The hostess seated them at the far end of the porch, at a small table overlooking a large pasture bounded by hardwoods where several horses grazed. The bucolic scene reminded River of her grandparents' farm, and for an instant, she felt a tinge of homesickness.

"Something wrong?"

Clay must have noticed her change of mood. She shook her head and smiled as she settled the napkin across her lap. "The view just reminded me of something, that's all."

"Something sad?"

"No, actually, something happy."

Just then a young, cheerful woman showed up at the table.

"Hi, Clay, you haven't been here in forever." She turned to River. "Hello."

"River, this is Preston's baby sister, Gwen."

Preston seemed to be close to their age, probably in his early thirties. Gwen looked much younger.

"I know what you're thinking and it's not true. I wasn't an accident." Gwen put her hand on her hip proudly. "Mama said she needed one more baby before she was too old to have one, so here I am."

River still wasn't used to the South, where people shared personal details whether you wanted to hear them or not and seemed to expect the same from you. Clay laughed.

"I'm sure River wasn't gonna ask your age."

"She was curious though. I could tell by the look on her face. Was I right?" She held a small spiral pad in one hand and pointed at River with the pen in her other.

"I admit I was curious."

"See? Told ya." She put pen to paper, poised to write. "Now, can I get y'all a drink?"

They ordered two glasses of red wine, and River let Clay order food for them. Clay knew the menu, and there were a couple of dishes she wanted River to try. She had the distinct feeling that sitting across the small table from Clay was going to dampen her appetite, but she agreed to sample whatever Clay ordered.

The black dress shirt was open just enough to reveal the occasional glimpse of Clay's collarbone, and River thought more than once about how she'd love the chance to trail soft kisses down Clay's neck to that delicious hollow space.

"So, tell me the story of River. I know so little about you that I'm beginning to wonder if you're part of some witness protection program." Clay smiled playfully at River over the rim of her wine glass. "You said earlier this place reminded you of something."

Clay paid attention. She got extra points for that.

"I was reminded of my grandparents' farm in upstate New York. They had a lot of land and horses. Although I wasn't the best at riding them. I got thrown off quite a few times." River looked out at the green field thinking back. "I don't think they respected my authority as a rider."

"I find that hard to believe."

"Why?"

"You seem very confident. I would definitely follow your directions. I take direction well."

River's cheeks heated. She was pretty sure Clay was no longer talking about horses.

"Now, I find that hard to believe." River took a sip of water to cool off. "I would have figured you for the loner type, adverse to authority."

"Not in all circumstances."

Clay had the urge to pinch herself to confirm she wasn't dreaming. She was trying not to flirt so obviously, but where River was concerned she couldn't seem to help herself. River looked so damn sexy sitting across from her.

She leaned away from the table as a young man from the kitchen helped Gwen deliver several plates of food. Clay glanced up to see River's wide-eyed appraisal of the culinary display and considered that maybe she'd ordered too much. She was nervous, and she'd probably overcompensated by ordering more than they could possibly eat.

"Where was their farm?" Clay served some food onto a share plate for River. Then did the same for herself.

"I grew up in the North Country, just south of Canton. Are you familiar with northern New York State?"

"Not really. I never made it farther than upstate. I drove up to Syracuse once with a friend for a party at the university. My friend was dating a woman who was in grad school there."

"Most people assume New York City is all there is to New York, but the city is at the very bottom corner of a huge state that is mostly rural. Beautiful green rolling hills, and then there's also the Adirondacks. That area is really pretty."

"How did you end up moving to the city?"

"I studied at NYU, and…well…I just sort of fell in love with the city and stayed. You said yourself that New York City is where you need to be if you want to immerse yourself in art."

"I did, didn't I?" Clay chewed for a moment. "Where does that leave me?"

"On sabbatical."

Clay laughed.

"You're an optimist."

"Absolutely." River reached for a second serving of fried green tomatoes.

"You like those, huh?"

"I didn't expect to, but they're really good." River shook her head.

"What?"

"There are a lot of unexpected things to like about the South."

River gazed intently at her from across the half-filled plates of food scattered around the small table. She held Clay with her eyes, causing warmth to flood her system.

"People from elsewhere are always making wrong assumptions about the South."

"Well, as your friend Trip said, you don't know until you know."

Clay laughed, reminded of their first meal at the diner and River's revelation about chicken fried steak.

"Tell me something else about yourself, River Hemsworth."

It seemed River wasn't the sort of woman to reveal personal details freely, but when asked, she shared openly. Clay liked

River's style. She was reserved initially, but open and friendly in conversation. River also didn't try to act like she was perfect or that she knew everything—traits commonly attributed to Northerners by Southerners. Clay oft times felt like a cross-cultural ambassador because she'd lived in both worlds.

"What would you like to know?"

"Do you come from a big family? Do you have siblings?"

"One brother, John. He's four years older and still lives in the North Country."

"He's not a city boy?"

"Far from it. He hates the city. I think he's only come to visit me a couple of times the entire time I've been there." River sipped her wine. Her silverware lay at the side of her mostly empty plate. "His wife, Maggie, would probably love to visit more often, if for no other reason than to shop."

"Do you like his wife?"

"Maggie's great. And she's perfect for John. She never pressures him to be anything other than who he is. She's also a solid helpmate on the farm, which really is a group, family effort most days. They moved into my grandparents' place after my grandfather passed away."

Helpmate was such an old-fashioned word. River's use of it amused her.

"What's funny?"

"Helpmate. That sounds like something from a Christian handbook about marriage."

"It probably is. The community I grew up in was super conservative. That's partly why I left and, I recently discovered, that's why my aunt left too."

River leaned forward. The position shift gave Clay an alluring view of cleavage. It required willpower not to lose the thread of the conversation and remain focused on River's face. Too late. She was fairly sure River caught her staring.

"See something interesting?"

"No, I mean, yes…what do you mean?" Busted.

Clay blushed and River decided to give her a break. River was flattered by the attention. She smiled and casually leaned back in the chair holding her wine glass in front of her. Finally, Clay smiled and laughed softly. River took a sip of her wine.

"Did I tell you my aunt left me a letter?"

"No, you didn't mention it."

"In the letter my aunt basically said the same thing. That she left because she knew she was a lesbian and there was no place for her there. And I guess my dad had a problem with his sister being gay. I can kind of see it now because he always seemed to struggle with my sexuality."

"Are your parents still…" Clay didn't finish the question.

"No, it's just my brother and me. I should probably call him. I don't think he has any idea I'm down here. He's not a big talker so we don't speak that often."

Gwen seemed to appear out of nowhere. Or maybe River had been so focused on Clay that she just hadn't noticed her surroundings for the past hour, or had it been two?

"Are you all finished here? I can get rid of these plates."

Clay nodded. "Thanks."

Gwen returned quickly with dessert menus.

Clay gave River a questioning look.

"Oh, none for me, thanks." River didn't think she could eat one more bite.

"Thanks, Gwen, we'll just take the check."

They were quiet for a minute, then Clay broke the silence.

"You were really a good passenger on the way over here, by the way. Not everyone is, you know." Clay finished her wine. "Some people don't know to lean into the curves."

"My brother had a dirt bike. I used to ride with him, and on rare occasions I'd sneak off and ride it by myself."

"Why did you have to sneak off to ride it?"

"Because my father was very into gender specific roles for his kids." River felt the familiar rise of frustration as she remembered her childhood and how she'd chafed at being forced into a role she didn't always want to play. "Girls didn't ride dirt bikes, in his opinion."

"Too bad. I'll bet you were good at it." Clay leaned forward with an earnest expression. "I'll bet you're good at anything you set your mind to."

Now River was sure she was blushing. Her cheeks warmed beneath the compliment.

"So, why did Trip call you Paintball?" She wanted to shift the conversation away from herself.

"Oh, geez...I can't believe you remember that." Clay laughed. "It's a nickname from a long time ago, back when we were in junior high."

"Because you like to paint?"

"No, not that kind of paint. I got trounced by a girl in a game of paintball. Massacred is more like it."

"She must have been cute."

"I thought so. She was my first crush, Suzan, with a z."

"Classy." River loved teasing Clay. It was almost too easy.

"Yeah, something like that."

Clay paid the check and they rode back in the dark to Pine Cone. The moon lit the treetops on either side of the two-lane highway. They passed hardly any cars on the way home. Clay had obviously chosen a less-traveled, scenic route. River focused on taking in the journey.

On a motorcycle, everything was more intense. They passed a pond and she noticed right away the microclimate, the cooled air near the water. And the night air smelled so good, of fresh cut grass, and a bonfire somewhere in the distance. Riding behind Clay, she was fully exposed to the nighttime world.

Once again, the twenty-minute ride seemed shorter.

Clay parked the bike and followed River to the front door. Before she put the key in the lock, River turned to face Clay. River wasn't going to wait for Clay to make the first move; she'd wanted to kiss Clay all night. Every time Clay touched her tongue to her lips it was as if she were teasing River from across the table.

River angled her head and pressed Clay's mouth firmly against hers. She parted her lips and took Clay in. The swirling, dizzying contact carried just a hint of red wine. Clay stepped closer, until River's back was pressed against the door. Clay's hand was drifting precariously close to her breast, and she brushed it aside. She felt Clay smile against her mouth, breaking the kiss. Luckily, River had forgotten to leave the porch light on, so there wasn't enough light on the scene for the neighborhood to witness their scandalous good night at the front door.

"Let's go inside."

"I don't think that's a very good idea."

Clay swept her hand up the outside curve of River's breast, and River held on to it this time, raising Clay's palm to her lips for a light kiss.

"Why?" Clay sounded a bit crestfallen.

"I'm not going to invite you in on a first date."

"Second date…no wait, third date." Clay brushed an errant strand of hair off River's cheek with her fingertip. She'd put no space between them, and River could feel the warmth of Clay's breath on her skin. "What about the other night? Pineapple casserole night?"

"That was a social call, remember? You stopped by to check on my car." River's hand drifted down the front of Clay's shirt.

"What about last night?"

"We bumped into each other at the downtown market. Officially, *not* a date."

"Even with a sunset, moonlight, and Elvis?"

River shook her head.

"Wow, I can see I have to up my game."

"A date is when you call a woman and take her out. Tonight was our first date."

Clay let her hands drop slowly to River's hips where she applied pressure, drawing her closer. River closed her eyes and moaned softly.

"I think you want to invite me in," Clay whispered.

River smiled and tipped her forehead against Clay's soft lips.

"Yes, I do." She placed her hand in the center of Clay's chest. It took every ounce of self-control she could muster to put space between them. "Which is why, Clay Cahill, you are not coming in this house with me."

Clay looked adorably incredulous standing in the moonlight. And for a split second, River considered breaking her cardinal rule: no sex on a first date. But that rule had saved her before and it might just be saving her now. She wanted more from Clay than hormones whipped into a frenzy after one dinner out. She wanted more time with Clay, and she was fairly sure this was one way to get it.

She closed the space between them, kissed Clay softly on the lips, and turned to unlock the door. She looked back one more time before she closed it.

"Good night, Clay."

Chapter Eighteen

Clay sat slouched in the old rolling office chair with her eyes closed, basking in the warmth of the morning sun streaming through the dusty front window of the garage. She'd woken up feeling light and changed somehow. With her eyes closed, she could almost conjure the sensation of River's lips on hers, the press of her body, the scent of her skin. Clay exhaled slowly.

A shadow pulled her from the trance.

River stood in the doorway, looking, as usual, like perfection itself in shorts and a simple cotton blouse. It was as if Clay had conjured her out of thin air. A slow smile spread across River's face.

"Hello." The chair squeaked as Clay leaned forward. This was a very pleasant surprise.

"Hi." River walked to the desk as Clay stood up. "I brought you some coffee and something sweet." She held the bag open for Clay. Three coffees were perched in a cardboard tray in her other hand.

"You mean something sweet besides you?"

"You're good."

"I can turn on some charm when the occasion calls for it." Clay peeked into the bag. "Cinnamon rolls, my favorite."

"MJ has ruined me. Ever since I had that giant cinnamon bun at the B and B I've had a craving for them."

"I've been having a craving for other things ever since last night." Clay smiled around a mouthful of pastry and frosting.

"Yeah, me too." River leaned her shoulder into Clay playfully.

"Wait, there are three coffees here. Are you trying to flirt with someone else here at Cahill Auto Repair?"

"Hello there! Don't let this one give you a hard time now." Clay's grandpa strode through the door from the repair shop to the office.

"Grandpa, this is Eve's niece, River." Clay took a respectable step back, giving River some space.

"Very nice to meet you, Mr. Cahill." River extended her hand, and Clay's grandpa took it in both of his, clasping with one and patting the back of her hand with the other.

"What can we do for you on this fine day? I'm afraid we haven't been able to salvage your car, but I heard the Clip 'n Curl is back on her feet and feeling fine since the bust up."

River laughed. "I'm glad to hear I didn't cause any lasting damage." She held one of the coffees out to him. "I took the liberty of bringing you a coffee and something to eat from the bakery."

"Well, now, I like this gal, Clay." He accepted the bag containing the last pastry along with the coffee. "Any woman who'll feed you is high on my list."

"And he has a refrigerator full of casserole dishes to prove it."

He gave her a playful scowl as she finished off the last bite of the cinnamon roll.

"If you're going to be here for a little while I'll take a break outside with River."

"I'll be here, enjoying my fancy coffee. You gals go take a walk. It's a beautiful day. Someone ought to be out there enjoying it." He dropped into the chair Clay had previously occupied.

Clay held the door for River. Just as they crossed the threshold, Bo came out of nowhere rolling a tire toward the bay door.

"Oh, sorry." River stepped back out of his way bumping into Clay.

"No problem." He slowed and gave River a full body scan. Then he stopped completely and extended his hand.

"Well, hello. The name is Bo." That was the most charm Clay had ever seen him display and, at that moment, made him about as popular as a snake in a sleeping bag.

"Hi, I'm—"

"She's just dropping off some coffee."

"None for me?"

He was still holding his hand out, either in greeting or waiting for something else, Clay wasn't sure. She'd never seen Bo so attentive, especially this early in the morning. River looked down at his palm, covered with black from the new tire. Clay stepped around River.

"Any day now, Bo," Eddie called from several feet way.

Bo frowned, then looked back at River and smiled. "Another time."

Clay glared at him as she steered River by the elbow toward a weathered picnic table on the far side of the parking lot near an ancient payphone booth. An empty plastic cover dangled where a phone book used to reside.

"Who was that?" River glanced back toward the garage once they were seated.

"Bo Mathis, local asshole."

"And he works here?"

"Not for long, I hope."

"Despite your subtlety, I take it you don't like him."

"No."

"He doesn't like you either." It was a statement, rather than a question, as if River already knew the whole story just from one, brief encounter.

"Perceptive."

"Why doesn't he like you?"

"It's a long story that I'd rather not burden you with." Clay reached across the table and teased River's fingers with hers until River loosely entwined their fingers. "I'd rather talk about other things with you."

"Last night was really nice."

"It was hard to say good night. I considered sleeping on your doorstep just to be near you." The truth was Clay thought of knocking on the door and talking her way into the house, into River's bed. But they'd had a perfect evening, and Clay hadn't wanted to spoil it by rushing something she wasn't even sure she was ready for. They'd kissed and said good night at the door. That's what happened on a date, right?

"What a coincidence, because it was incredibly hard not to invite you in."

"Now you tell me." Clay smiled and caressed the back of River's hand with her thumb.

River turned Clay's hand over and traced the lines of her palm lightly with her fingertip. The faintest touch and yet it tingled all the way up her arm.

"Do you enjoy working at a garage? Driving a tow truck?"

Clay shrugged.

"You'd really rather do this than paint?" River didn't sound judgmental, simply curious.

"Not much for small talk, are you?"

"No, not really. Not if I really want to know someone."

"I've always liked cars." Clay sipped her latte. "I used to hang out here a lot when I was a kid. This garage was like a second home."

"So, it's a safe space for you?"

"Well, it sounds kinda woo-woo and politically correct when you say it that way, but yes, it's a safe space."

River laughed. "Sorry, I seriously didn't mean to be politically correct."

They were quiet for a moment. A car drove past, braked, and turned at the corner. Country music blared through the open window as it passed.

"Are you afraid to paint?" River spoke with tenderness in her voice.

"Yeah, I'm afraid." Exposing her inner self to the world again was not high on Clay's list. Especially a world she'd recently discovered she couldn't trust. The business of art seemed exploitive and hurtful, the opposite of what it should be, in her opinion. Maybe River was different, but Clay didn't know her well enough to be sure of that. Not yet anyway. "You don't know what it's like."

"You're right. I don't know what it's like, but I would give anything to have the talent you have. To be able to make people feel something. Your images are so powerful. That's a rare gift."

Clay wondered if River was overstating things, but she seemed genuinely serious about the assessment of Clay's work. She held Clay with her eyes and squeezed her hand for emphasis.

"Maybe I'll feel it again." Clay placed her palm over the center of her chest. "But this...this right here...isn't ready to be hanging on some wall in some gallery. Not yet."

Clay considered inviting River to the cookout at Trip's house later that day. Was that too much? She was a little afraid to integrate River too soon into her "friend" circle, Clay's other safe space. But there'd be lots of people around. Nothing could get too serious with a crowd around.

"Hey, there's a cookout at Trip's house later today. Would you like to go?"

"Trip mentioned it to me yesterday. I was considering it, but I wasn't sure I wanted to show up by myself." She paused. "I'd love to go with you."

"Oh, she already asked you." Clay was a little surprised that Trip had invited River without checking with her. Was Trip trying to set her up again?

"Yes, but I wouldn't have gone without talking with you first. I know you and Trip are close and, well, I wouldn't want to just show up at your friend's house without discussing it with you."

River had boundaries. Good to know.

"You should join me. I mean, you should come. I mean, I can give you a ride." Clay was struggling. Every statement she made sounded like it had some sexual double meaning. She was sure she was blushing because her cheeks suddenly warmed as did other parts. "What I meant to say is I could come pick you up when I'm finished here. Would four thirty be okay for you?"

"I think I know what you mean." River was smiling, her eyes sparkled. Which part was she smiling about? "I'll see you at four thirty."

Clay walked River to her old pickup and opened the door for her.

"Thanks." River cranked the truck. "I'll look forward to seeing you later."

Clay sauntered backward toward the office. She dragged her foot every other step, not wanting to turn around until River was out of sight. Man, her stomach was in knots. Four thirty couldn't get there soon enough.

"That River is an attractive young woman." Her grandpa didn't lower the newspaper he was reading or look at her as he spoke.

"Yeah, I noticed."

"Nice too. And polite."

"Yeah, she is." Clay leaned against the counter looking out the front window of the office.

"You gonna see her again any time soon?" He noisily turned the page, which he obviously wasn't reading.

"I'm picking her up this afternoon. She's going with me to a cookout at Trip's house."

"Good. Maybe she can cheer you up." Finally, he looked up and winked.

"Yeah, maybe so."

He folded the paper, stood, and stretched his back.

"You know, life doesn't just hand you things. Sometimes you have to make an effort if you want things to change. If you want good things to come your way." He downed the last of his to-go coffee and tossed the cup in the trash. "There's nothing free in this world but the grace of God."

"I'll have to weigh that." Clay rested her chin in her hand.

"You weigh it. You'll see that I'm right." He patted her shoulder on his way to the door. "All right then, I'm gonna go check on Edith Miller. She called earlier to invite me over to sample some peach cobbler."

"Sounds like a mission worthy of your skills. Tell Mrs. Miller I said hello."

Her grandpa waved but didn't turn around as his slightly stooped frame was silhouetted by the morning sun in the doorway. He ambled toward his truck, looking left and right and casting a wave in Eddie's direction.

Clay wondered what life felt like for her grandpa. He was happy and he seemed to have it all figured out now that he was in his twilight years. Did he ever have the desire to go back and do things differently? Or did forbearance come with age? Clay wondered if she'd always look back at her time in New York with regrets, or if some day she'd actually move beyond it. Everyone made mistakes. Why couldn't she move past hers?

"She's a little out of your league, ain't she?"

Clay had been lost in thought until she heard Bo's voice.

"None of your business. You need to steer clear of me and of River."

"Is that a warning?" He poured himself a coffee and glanced sideways at her.

"More like a promise."

"Hmm." He sipped his coffee and stared off as if he were pondering the mysteries of the universe.

She was about to say something else, but then the phone rang and Bo weaseled back to the garage while she answered it.

Chapter Nineteen

R iver stopped halfway up the driveway, leaning forward for a better view. Trip's house looked like a Southern mansion. A long, wide driveway entered the property and then split off to the left where the house sat a good distance off the road. To the right of the drive was a quaint Victorian with a sign that identified it as the vet clinic. Beyond that, she could see a long, U-shaped stable ringed by paddocks and a riding ring complete with jumps. Wow. This was an impressive spread.

The private residence was separated from the clinic and stables by a dark board fence and an iron gate guarded by a butch woman who was checking IDs and reading a short list of rules to each guest before letting them past. She directed most cars to parking in a grassed area behind a huge old barn past the house, but after reading the rules—including a warning that she must pass a breathalyzer to drive out—and checking a clipboard, she directed River to park with the handful of cars on the front lawn. She wondered if she'd been awarded VIP parking.

Clay had called around three thirty to say she had a request for a tow that she had to take care of so River should go ahead to Trip's and Clay would meet her there. But now she really regretted not telling Clay she'd simply wait for her so that they could arrive together.

The party seemed to be in full swing when River arrived. A steady stream of cars, trucks, and a higher than average number of Subarus clogged the drive, many honking their horns as they drove past the huge crowd of women overflowing the backyard to park behind the barn. Yes, she was definitely at a lesbian gathering. It felt oddly intimate to be driving up to Clay's best friend's house in Clay's truck. She parked and followed two other women who'd also apparently rated VIP parking in the front. They politely nodded hello as they crossed the neatly trimmed lawn to the front of the house.

Luckily, Trip was greeting people in the foyer.

"River. Hey there. So glad you could make it." Trip motioned her over. "Come on, I'll show you where the drinks are and then we'll get you some food. Where's Clay?"

"She had a late call, but she said she'll be here for sure." River followed Trip as they wound their way through the living room and out double French doors to the patio and pool area. "Trip, your house is amazing." She'd gotten used to small spaces in the city. She couldn't imagine having this much room to breathe.

"Thanks. I have to tell you that I can't really take credit for it. I inherited this place from my grandfather."

"Well, it's beautiful."

There were bartending stations at each end of the pool. River had brought along a bottle of champagne and, unsure what to do with it, handed it over to Trip.

"Would you like me to open this for you?"

"That'd be great, thank you." River watched as Trip removed the foil and aimed the bottle in a safe direction to pop the cork. "I wasn't sure what to bring."

"This is a good choice. We've got quite a few women here who like the bubbly stuff. Personally, I like a nicely chilled pale ale." Trip snagged a plastic cup from the nearest bartender and filled it with champagne. "I know it's best in a glass flute, but I have a strict no-glass rule around the pool." She grabbed a marker from the table and wrote River's name on the champagne bottle, then handed it to the bartender, who plunged it into a deep plastic watering trough that was filled to the brim with ice and drinks. The bartender poured a pale ale into one of the red plastic cups and handed it to Trip.

"Here's to new friends." Trip tipped her glass in River's direction.

"To new friends." They clinked cups lightly and sipped.

"Well, now, you just mingle and make yourself at home. I left Jay to watch the grill, and if I know her she'll burn the burgers before I get back."

River took a few more sips and scanned the pool area. There was a table, shaded by a festively striped umbrella nearby with an empty chair. She decided to join the small group of women at the table and introduce herself. Plus, the chair afforded her a nice view of the house so she could keep an eye out for Clay.

Clay finally got to Trip's place around five thirty, later than she'd planned. After the last call of the day, she'd gone home, showered and changed, and then ridden her motorcycle to the cookout. She hoped River hadn't given up on her and left. She ran her fingers through her still damp hair as she scanned the crowd. She said hello to a couple of friends as she made her way toward the patio, where she paused and slowly panned the pool area. By the time she spotted her, River was already walking toward her. She was wearing an ivory dress that clung teasingly to every curve.

"Wow, you look fantastic."

"Thanks, so do you." River leaned in and gave Clay a friendly kiss on the cheek.

"I'm sorry it took me so long to get here. Have you made some new friends?"

"A few. People here are very friendly. But you were the *friend* I most wanted to see." River trailed her fingers down Clay's arm.

When River's fingers reached Clay's wrist, she rotated her hand and captured River's. She knew she'd never hear the end of it if Trip or Grace spotted them holding hands, but she didn't care.

"I'm starved. Have you eaten yet?"

"No, but I've scouted out our options. Burgers and quesadillas and some yummy looking chips and salsa." They angled toward the food tables hand in hand. Clay said hello to a couple of women who shot her questioning looks. She wasn't completely sure if they were interested in her or interested in River. Too late on either count, because Clay wasn't going to let River out of her sight for the rest of the night.

"Let's get a little of everything."

"Sounds good."

They heaped two plates and then walked back toward the double French doors.

"Want to eat inside out of the heat? I wanted to see if Trip was inside too so I could say hello." Clay tipped her head toward the air-conditioned interior.

When they entered the living area, which opened directly into the dining and kitchen, the entire space overflowed with mostly women and a smattering of men drinking, eating, and competing to be heard.

"Oh, we forgot to get you a drink. What do you want and I'll get it for you?"

"I'll take a beer, thanks."

Trip walked up just as River stepped back outside.

"One little dance in the gazebo and she's already fetching you drinks?"

"She's polite that way." Clay bit off part of her quesadilla.

"Great turnout, Trip. Did you invite the whole damn town?"

"Most of it." Trip pulled Clay across the room toward a tall androgynous looking woman with ebony hair. The woman looked a little lost in the crowd. As they got closer, Clay recognized her. She'd seen this woman once before with Grace.

"Hey, I want you to meet someone." The dark-haired woman looked up as Trip approached, with Clay in tow. "Hi, Dani, Glad you could make it." Trip patted Dani on the back. "I was beginning to wonder if you were going to blow me off."

Trip jerked her thumb toward Clay. "Don't think you've been properly introduced, but this is Clay Cahill, resident artist extraordinaire and part-time tow truck driver and grease monkey."

Clay shifted her paper plate loaded with a burger, quesadillas, chips and salsa to her left hand and offered a half wave. "Welcome to Pine Cone and the best cookout in the county."

"Thanks. Nice to meet you too."

"There's River. I'm going to go relieve her of that nice cold beer."

Clay cut through the crowded room, leaving Trip to chat with Dani. Clay didn't really enjoy balancing food and a drink while standing, but there were no seats to be had so they made the best of it, by leaving their drinks on a nearby windowsill so they could more easily hold the plate with one hand and eat with the other. River seemed completely entertained by Clay's food juggling act and people watching. Somehow, River managed to make standing and eating look effortless. Clay admired River's poise, regardless of the situation.

"So, you dressed up for this cookout, huh?"

"What? This?" River looked down at the dress. "Not really." She tugged the hem out a little in invitation. "Feel it. It's made of stretchy cotton T-shirt material. This dress is actually cooler and more comfortable than shorts."

"Hmm, I stand corrected." Clay quirked an eyebrow as she fingered the fabric. "You wear it well."

"Almost as good as you wear those Levi's."

Clay almost choked on a chip. Before she could recover, Grace entered her peripheral vision and she looked upset. Dani, the woman Clay had met just a few minutes earlier, was tugging Grace by the arm toward the hallway.

"Sorry, will you excuse me just a minute?"

Clay pushed through the crowd in an attempt to intercept.

"Are you okay, Grace?" Clay was just about to reach for Dani, but Grace waved her off. Clay watched them disappear down the hallway before she returned to River.

"Is everything all right?"

"Yeah, I was just checking on Grace."

"You two are close, aren't you?"

"We are. I love Grace like a sister."

"And you…you were never…"

"Together? Only once, for about four minutes."

"Four whole minutes?"

Clay laughed. "Yes, we kissed under the bleachers one night after a football game back when we were in high school. And then we decided we were much better as friends."

"Lucky for me." River smiled mischievously. They finished their food and Clay led River back outside.

Clay motioned toward a couple of open chairs by the pool, she was ready to sit for a while and enjoy her beer. "Before I sit down I'm going to make a quick run to the restroom. Save my seat." There was a small table between two lounge chairs where River deposited her drink and cell phone. Clay relaxed, sipped her beer, and watched several bikini clad women splash each other on the other side of the pool. Trip was grilling a second round of food and entertaining a small circle of women as she cooked. Clay couldn't make out what Trip was saying, but it was obviously entertaining. The women surrounding Trip were laughing and seemed to be hanging on her every word. Trip loved a rapt audience.

River's phone vibrated, causing it to dance against the metal poolside table. Clay glanced over absently, not meaning to pry, but she couldn't help noticing her name pop up in the text message that flashed across the screen. She leaned over for a closer look.

How's it going? Any luck landing Clay Cahill as a client? Inquiring minds are dying to know.

What the fuck? Clay sat bolt upright, every muscle suddenly tightly coiled. She should have followed her initial cautionary impulse and stayed the hell away from River. This was all happening again like a nightmarish loop she couldn't break free of. God, how could she be so stupid? Clay was angry, hurt, and disappointed in herself. All three feelings seemed stirred together into some toxic cocktail that triggered an impulse to flee, right that minute. She strode toward the French doors, cutting a quick path through the living room still crowded with people in random stages of inebriation, and in her blind fury almost ran right into River. She pulled up short, hardly able to even see her through the red haze of anger clouding her vision.

"Clay?"

Clay clenched her jaw. She didn't know what to say. She didn't want to say anything at all. She just wanted out. She wanted to be away.

"What's wrong? Are you leaving?"

The hurt, confused expression on River's face tugged at her insides, but not enough to stay. She'd seen the text. She knew the truth now. Regardless of how she'd thought she felt about River, or what she thought River felt about her, she'd been wrong. Again.

"Am I a date or a client?"

"What?"

"It doesn't matter." She surged forward, bumping into a woman who didn't get out of her way fast enough, and was out the door.

❖

Shocked, River watched the door close behind Clay.

What was Clay talking about?

Why would she ask if she was a client?

River puzzled over Clay's strange, abrupt, infuriating behavior as she walked back poolside to retrieve her phone. She glanced at the text from Amelia on the screen and instantly knew. She closed her eyes and pinched the bridge of her nose. *Fuck.* Clay had obviously seen the text from Amelia. A wave of queasiness threatened to capsize her so she dropped to the chair and waited for her stomach to settle.

She covered her mouth and scanned the festive party. She felt isolated from the joy all around her. She needed to fix this, but how? Should she follow Clay? Should she give Clay time to cool off? She had no idea what to do.

Chapter Twenty

R iver wracked her brain to pull up details of where Clay lived. They'd only stopped by there the one time and she wasn't sure she could find it. If she could remember the street they'd turned on then she thought she could find it. Surely there weren't that many livable warehouse spaces in Pine Cone.

"Hey, why are you sitting all by yourself over here?" Trip paused near her chair, on her way to deliver a plateful of burgers to the buffet table. "Where's Clay?"

"Um, something came up and I think she had to leave."

"She had to leave?"

River was no good at subterfuge, and she certainly didn't want to tell Trip the truth. She smiled weakly at Trip as she stood up. "Actually, I should get going also. Thank you so much for inviting me."

"Okay, well, when you see Clay tell her to call me. It's not like her to leave without saying good-bye." Trip seemed suspicious of River's explanation.

One more reason not to linger.

The champagne had given her a buzz, but not so much so that she couldn't pass the breathalyzer she was required to take before claiming her keys. Crossing the uneven grassy field to the truck proved more challenging. She almost turned her ankle before she settled herself in the driver's seat. Several deep breaths didn't calm her uneasiness as she backed out and turned the truck toward town. She's was desperate to explain things to Clay. This was a terrible, awful, huge misunderstanding.

❖

Clay stood in the middle of the large open space breathing hard. For the first time since leaving New York, she had too many feelings. The weight of them bore down on her, making her limbs feel heavy.

The canvas she'd drowned with black paint was still on the floor. She picked it up and slammed the edge of it against the nearest concrete support column until it cracked. Bracing the fractured wooden frame against her knee, she bent the painting in half and shoved it in the oversized trash can.

She returned to the shelves full of art supplies, pulled a large roll of canvas away from the wall, and unfurled it in one massive arcing move. The raw canvas was about ten feet square.

She kicked her shoes off as she walked toward the metal shelves stocked with paint. She scanned the colors for a moment but realized that red was the only option. The jar of brushes tipped over in her haste to grab for one, and she left them spilled across the table.

With the canister of liquid acrylic in one hand and the brush, like a weapon in the other, Clay approached the canvas like some big game hunter staging a kill. With deliberate, swift strokes, she began to throw color at the blank canvas, using the brush but without making contact. Liquid red pooled and spattered like some flayed animal in the throes of death. But there was too much distance and not enough contact.

She set the brush and paint aside, sank her hands into the wet paint, and swept them across the canvas in successive arcs. A tear escaped and trailed down her cheek. She brushed at it with the shoulder of her T-shirt. She was in it now, fully, completely. She turned again toward the shelving full of canisters with the sensation of paint slowly dripping from her fingers as if from a wound. She needed more. Something to kill the red.

❖

River slowed the truck and leaned forward to peer through the windshield. This looked like the street they'd taken to Clay's place. She wasn't completely sure, but there was only one way to find out. Three blocks down, she spotted Clay's motorcycle. This was the place. River switched off the engine and debated not going in. But she couldn't leave things unsaid. If she didn't face Clay now and explain, she'd be miserably awake all night thinking about what she should have done.

The door was ajar. Something told River not to knock. She nudged the door open. What she saw was the absolute last scene she'd expected to find. Clay was braced on one arm above a canvas on the floor, making broad strokes with her other hand. Red paint was splattered on her gray T-shirt and across one cheek as if she'd been cut. River swallowed, frozen in place, wanting to be seen and not seen at the same time.

Clay straightened and stood, looking down at the canvas. When she finally looked up, the unguarded emotion on her face caused River's heart to hurt. Instinctively, she brought her hand to her chest. Clay didn't move. Like some otherworldly creature surprised in the wild at night by passing headlights, she seemed rooted in place. Slowly, cautiously, River moved toward her. Clay edged around the canvas without taking her eyes off River, so that she stood between River and the image spread across the floor.

"What are you doing here, River?"

"I know you saw the text." Her voice faltered. "It's not what you think."

River stepped closer.

"Clay, I know you saw that message from Amelia. She doesn't know everything." River could see the hurt and anger on Clay's face. "When I first saw your paintings in my aunt's gallery, yes, I wanted to represent your work in my gallery, but not anymore."

Clay didn't respond.

"After the almost kiss and then two nights ago when we danced and then had dinner out. I knew I couldn't have you as a client. But I haven't gotten a chance to tell Amelia yet."

"Why don't you want me as a client?"

"Because…Clay…because I'm falling for you."

"River, I can't go through this again if—"

"Clay, let me show you how I feel." River cut her off. "Please."

Clay seemed to consider River's words, as if she were deciding whether to trust their sincerity. After a moment, Clay stepped closer.

Clay traced River's cheek with one finger and then gripped the back of River's neck beneath her hair. The intensity of Clay's gaze was as sharp as a blade. She didn't break eye contact until their lips met. River sank into Clay, allowing Clay to have her way. She felt Clay's hand at the small of her back, pressing their bodies together. Then Clay's hand drifted to the outer curve of her breast. River slipped her hands under the hem of Clay's T-shirt until she felt Clay's muscles twitch beneath her fingers. Only then did Clay pull back.

"I've ruined your dress." Clay looked at the palm of her once paint-covered hand and then back at the smears of paint on River's clothing. Like some living canvas, the ivory cotton dress was covered now with handprints.

"I don't care." River smiled up at Clay. "Come here."

River led Clay to the large white sink mounted on the wall. She stood between Clay and the sink as she ran the water to warm it. Then she pulled Clay's hand around her waist from behind her and began to wash away the paint by rubbing Clay's hand gently between hers. Carefully, she stroked each finger and Clay's palm beneath the running water until all the paint was gone. Then she pulled Clay's other hand forward to repeat the cleansing, which felt more intimate and sensual than she'd expected. Obviously, she wasn't the only one who felt the heat rising between them.

Clay pulled her hair to one side and teased with the tip of her tongue up River's neck to the outside edge of her ear. Chills rippled across her skin and she shivered. Then, as Clay placed light kisses down River's neck, she eased up the hem of River's dress with one hand. River turned off the water and braced both hands on the cool edge of the sink for fear that her legs could no longer support her under the power of Clay's touch.

Now Clay was using both hands to slide the fabric up over River's hips; she felt the brush of denim against her bare skin. With one finger, Clay followed the path of the narrow thong fabric down to the place between her legs. River inhaled sharply, she felt Clay's arm around her, her hand covering River's breast as Clay stroked the tapered strip of damp fabric between her legs.

She rotated in Clay's arms, pulled the casual dress, now covered in paint, up and over her head, tossing it aside. Clay kissed her shoulder as she slid the bra strap away. Then she slid her fingers under the silky fabric of her bra and caressed as she teased River's mouth with her tongue. River reached around and unfastened her bra, letting it fall away. She relieved Clay of her T-shirt to find that Clay was wearing nothing underneath. The thrill of Clay's breasts against hers was immediate and electric as she draped her arms around Clay's neck. She felt Clay's hands on her ass again, urging her up. Clay half lifted her, then held her as River wrapped her legs around Clay's waist and Clay carried her toward the bed, never breaking their kiss.

Clay dropped to her knees on the mattress on the floor at the far end of the large space and gently laid River on pillows. Then she sat back on her heels as recognition of what was happening registered on her face.

River reached for her hand, hoping to keep her from leaving again. She crossed the bed to Clay on her knees.

"Clay, please trust me. Let me make love to you."

Still kneeling in front of Clay, she took Clay's hand and guided it inside the satin triangle of her underwear. She was incredibly wet, and now Clay knew it too.

Clay was vaguely aware of the brush of River's fingers as she unbuckled her belt and worked the buttons of her jeans loose. It was hard to focus on anything but her own fingers touching River, caressing her, teasing her.

River lay back and pulled Clay with her. She settled between River's legs, raising up just enough to slide the thong off and toss it aside. Then she pulled River tightly against her so that she could feel River against her lower abdomen. River pushed Clay's jeans over her hips with her feet. Clay slid them down farther with her free hand and kicked them off.

There was nothing between them. No barriers except the walls Clay had been so carefully constructing. And now, the sensation of River's body beneath hers was quickly dismantling even those. River was pulling her in and pulling her down into some heated oblivion. They were joined, the two of them one flesh, rising to meet each other. River's mouth open against her neck, her nails digging into Clay's shoulder, urging her for more, deeper, faster, until she felt River tighten around her fingers and heard her cry out in release.

Only a moment passed, with Clay kissing River tenderly before River rolled her over, switching their positions. She straddled Clay's midsection, wet and warm against her stomach. Methodically, sensually, River slid down Clay's body, softly leaving kisses as she went. Across her chest, each breast, gently teased with her tongue before skimming her teeth lightly over the highly sensitive skin. Down she traveled, her hair tickling with a feather's touch across her stomach until River settled between her legs.

As the pressure grew, Clay filled her fingers with River's hair, a silent request for more. She fisted the sheet and writhed beneath River's insistent, relentless, heavenly mouth. Climbing until the air thinned, she held her breath, the razor-sharp edge of release cut through her, she was falling too, and only River was there to catch her.

Chapter Twenty-one

River slowly blinked. It was dark, Clay's warmth seeped in from the other side of the bed. Their bodies made light contact under the sheet, and River tried her best to move away without waking Clay. She finger-combed her tousled hair and squinted into the cavernous space.

She'd hardly taken in the room when she'd first arrived. All she could see in those first moments was Clay, splashed with red as if she'd been in a street fight. River glanced over at Clay. She was asleep, her lean body only half covered by the sheet. Faint moonlight from one of the skylights painted the contours of her hip bones and her long legs, outlined in relief through the thin fabric. Clay's body was androgynous perfection.

River searched around the bed for clothing and ended up pulling on Clay's T-shirt as she walked toward the sink. The concrete warehouse floor was cool under her bare feet. She filled a glass with water and slowly rotated to take in the room.

Art supplies, unpainted canvases, shelves full of paint, were stored all along the wall to her left. Across the opposite wall were four finished canvases. They weren't hanging, but instead rested on the floor, leaning against the wall. She stepped around the unfinished painting still spread across the floor from earlier and stopped in front of the four canvases.

The compositions were barely lit by the moon from nearby windows and in the shadows, took on an ethereal aura.

River wasn't sure how long she'd been standing there when she felt Clay's hand slip under the too-large T-shirt. Her fingers slid across River's stomach and those muscles quivered from her touch.

"You're not sleeping."

"I was thirsty."

Clay took the glass from her hand and drank. She walked in front of River, her gaze intense. Clay kneeled in front of her, setting the glass on the floor.

"What are you doing?"

"This." Clay lifted the hem of the shirt and kissed the low curve of River's stomach, the lowest spot just above her dark curls.

River caressed Clay's hair and tried not to sway on her feet. Clay moved her hands to River's hips, holding her in place as she began to explore with her tongue.

"Clay, if you do that, right now…I'm never going to be able to look at your paintings again without thinking of—"

"Good." Clay looked up briefly and smiled. "When you look at my canvases I don't want you to think of anything else."

River stood, a glorious captive of Clay's hands. The muscles in her legs tensed and reflexively, she spread them farther apart. Her eyes had been closed as she allowed herself to swim in the sensation of Clay's gifted, intoxicating tongue between her legs. Until, in the instant of her liberation, she opened her eyes, Clay's paintings filled her vision with color and motion. She almost collapsed backward as she tipped over the cliff, but Clay was there, her strong hands moving up River's back as she stood. She guided River into her arms, with one arm under her pliant knees, and carried her back to bed.

❖

The coffee cups clattered in Clay's hand. She glanced over to the bed, but River didn't stir. The sun was streaming in at odd angles cutting across the large open room, from the skylight, and from a row of windows high on the front and back wall. She stood for a moment and watched the shafts of light intersect each other, creating rainbow patterns on the floor.

It was around nine o'clock, and sunlight had not yet found the bed. It had taken Clay a week of dragging the mattress around to different spots in the large space before she found the sweet spot. The one small section of the floor where the sun didn't shine until after ten. It was like sleeping on a sundial.

Clay checked the fridge while the coffee brewed. The only real option was eggs. Oh, and one bagel that they'd have to split.

She noticed movement out of the corner of her eye. River shifted, yawned, and stretched. Clay had boxers and a T-shirt on, but River was still wearing only a sheet, and even that fell to her waist when she sat up and scanned the room. Her eyes were heavy-lidded from sleep and her hair was adorably tousled. Her cheeks had a bit more color than the day before. If she was embarrassed to have Clay see her in her birthday suit, she gave no indication of it. River rubbed her eyes with her palms and then squinted in Clay's direction.

"What time is it?"

"Around nine." Clay poured coffee, added cream, and brought the steaming mugs back to the rumpled bed. "Do you need sugar in this?"

River shook her head. "Thank you so much." She took one of the cups from Clay and examined it, smiling, before she tasted the coffee. "I love Depression-era dishware."

River answered Clay's unasked question.

"Oh. The way you looked at that I wasn't sure what you were doing. I'm glad to know my tableware passes inspection. Now, if I just had a table."

River laughed at Clay's joke about her sparsely appointed living quarters.

"Who needs a table when you have a mattress on the floor?"

Now it was Clay's turn to laugh.

"I should warn you, I'm not much of a morning person." River took another drink of her coffee.

"Me either." Clay braced on one elbow on top of the covers.

River was sitting up, with bent knees. She seemed to remember she had nothing on and drew the sheet up and held it in front of her chest.

"Don't cover up on my account." Clay gazed at River over the rim of her cup.

River swatted at Clay. She set the coffee on the floor next to the bed and fell backward into the pillows. She covered her face with her hands.

"What did we do last night?" River uncovered one eye and turned to Clay.

"Pretty much everything."

"Well, not everything."

"Really? What did we leave out?"

River laughed.

Clay set her coffee aside and River wiggled across the bed, snuggling into Clay's shoulder. She was still under the covers while Clay was on top. The sheet rose and fell with the curve of River's hip. Beautiful. She brushed her fingers through River's hair and then kissed her forehead.

"Does this surprise you?" Clay asked.

"Which part?"

"That we made love?"

"No, that doesn't surprise me." River kissed the sensitive spot just below her ear and then nuzzled there with her nose.

"Really?"

"Clay, the first time I saw you climb out of that tow truck I knew I was in trouble."

"And then I was kind of a jerk when I drove you to the B and B." She kissed River's forehead again. "I'm sorry about that."

"It's forgotten, besides…I think you've more than made up for it." River propped up on her elbow and looked at her. "And, Clay, you started painting again."

"Yeah. It felt good."

It was true. And that was probably the biggest, unexpected change. She'd started to paint again. A compulsion to express herself that she was finally unable to ignore. Not painting had left her feeling so empty, so alone. As if she'd lost her voice entirely. Last night was the first time since returning from New York that she'd been able to put something on canvas that felt true, pure. She had River to thank for that. But it was too early to delve too deeply into her creative psyche just now. There were other things on her mind.

"Are you hungry?" Clay tilted her head up and kissed River affectionately.

"I hate to admit this after everything we sampled during the cookout yesterday, but, yes."

"I'm sure those calories are long gone."

"You did try to test the limits of my stamina." River's hand rested in the center of Clay's chest. She moved her fingers a little, and Clay felt it all the way to her toes.

It seemed impossible, but Clay was still incredibly turned on.

"Do you have things you need to do today?" Clay asked.

"Not really, why?"

"I was thinking I could make us some breakfast and then… we could go back to bed."

"Oh, really?" River tilted her head up just enough to quirk an eyebrow at Clay. "Is that what you were thinking?"

River moved her hand from Clay's chest to her stomach and then slipped her fingers inside the front of Clay's boxers.

"Hmm, seems like maybe we should eat breakfast after."

Clay groaned. "We're definitely eating after if you keep doing that."

River stilled her fingers and slowly removed them from Clay's shorts.

"Two things first. I need to pee…and I need a toothbrush."

Clay smiled. She'd already brushed her teeth before River woke up. She pointed to an alcove on the far end of the room. There were partial walls but no door.

"Your landlord couldn't spring for a door?"

"Don't worry, I won't look. And there's a new toothbrush in the drawer next to the sink."

River started to get up and pull the sheet along with her, but Clay was still lying on top of it. Clay shook her head, smiling.

"You're incorrigible. Fine." River got up and walked to the bathroom, swaying her hips and giving Clay an excellent view of her firm, shapely ass.

As promised, Clay rolled over onto her side facing the wall. After a few minutes, she heard running water and then another minute later the mattress shifted with River's weight as she spooned against Clay's back.

"Now, where was I?" River bit Clay's ear teasingly and slipped her arm around Clay's waist and let her hand drift lower, until…

Clay rolled onto her back. River swept her fingers through Clay's hair and kissed her deeply, fiercely. Clay didn't want River to stop what she was doing with her fingers, but she wanted, needed, less clothing between them. She pushed her boxer shorts down and off. River shifted partially on top of her, tugging Clay's shirt up. River kissed her chest. Clay swept the T-shirt over her head, and in one power move, put River on her back. She pressed River's hands into the mattress over her head. They were both breathing hard already.

Her face was close to River's now, but she didn't make contact. She closed her eyes and drew in the scent she'd come to know as River's. She allowed her full weight to settle between River's legs. River began to arch into her. Clay's sole focus became giving River what she wanted. How she wanted it. As hard as she wanted it.

They moved together, rhythm and velocity increasing the closer they got to the edge. Until there was nowhere left to go, no air to breathe, only the weight of desire kept Clay from floating away entirely. She collapsed on top of River, heart racing, spent. There was no world aside from this bed and the heavenly body beneath hers.

Chapter Twenty-two

It was early afternoon by the time River left Clay. She was afraid if she didn't force herself to leave she might very well stay in bed with Clay all day, possibly forever. She dropped her keys on the table at her aunt's house, feeling sleep-deprived. She needed a hot shower and a nap. Or maybe a cold shower and a nap.

Warm water streamed over her sensitive skin. She leaned with outstretched arms against the cool tile and tilted her neck from one side to the other stretching and relaxing the muscles in her neck. She slid her hands over her wet hair and reached for shampoo.

She stood with the bottle in her hand, water streaming over her shoulders, frozen. Sadness passed over like a cloud across the sun, and she had to fight the urge not to cry.

She knew she needed to return to New York, but she'd realized just now that she didn't want to leave. Damn. Now what was she going to do?

Staying wasn't really an option, so, decision made.

She'd make the most of her time left with Clay. Surely Clay knew she had to leave. River had a life in the city she needed to get back to. Sooner rather than later. It wasn't as if they couldn't still see each other. But her thoughts circled back to the revelation again. She needed to go back, but she didn't want to.

She rinsed the shampoo out of her hair and turned off the water. Sleep was what she needed. She was simply tired and not thinking clearly. A few hours of sleep and everything would start making sense again. Her brain's circuits were frayed by too much exquisite sex.

If she'd just had the best sex ever, why was she feeling so sad?

River pulled a clean T-shirt over her head and sank to the edge of the bed.

Was it possible that she'd been sad all along and not known it? There was so much about her life in the North Country that she loved, and missed. She'd closed the door on that part of her life, partly out of anger over her father's conservatism, the community as a whole. She'd never really allowed herself to mourn the loss of what had been good about her past there. And she'd always assumed that there was no way to recapture that life and be who she was at the same time. Thus, New York City had become her life. But now, well, she was starting to see another possibility. Maybe seeing another path, that there were other options, maybe this allowed her to miss the life she'd left behind. A charming small-town existence where neighbors cared about neighbors. A place where people truly knew you, your history, your dreams, you. The barista who scribbled her name on a paper cup each morning at the trendy café in Chelsea didn't really know her, not like that anyway.

She wasn't dismissing her life in New York, there were a lot of things to love about it, but it was possible that she'd let the glamour and excitement of it all block the panorama in the rearview mirror of where she'd come from. All the things that made River who she was. Being in Pine Cone, being with Clay, parts of it were coming back. What did that mean? And what was she going to do about it?

As she lay back on the cool sheets, her body was overwhelmed by the sensation of Clay's hands moving over her skin. Like a phantom limb that could still be felt once removed, the imprint of Clay on her flesh engulfed her senses. She pressed her palms to her eyes to hold in the tears. Vanquished, she let the sobs come.

River finally roused around five o'clock, famished, only to find cheese, crackers, and a sad looking apple left over from her last grocery run. Well, that would have to do because in her current mood and state of undress she wasn't venturing to the Piggly Wiggly. She was standing in the kitchen in only her T-shirt and underwear as she dialed Amelia's number.

"River, you never texted me back." Amelia sounded a little hurt.

"Sorry, I was indisposed…"

"With?"

"I'll give you two guesses and the first one doesn't count."

"Clay."

"Yeah." River sighed and leaned against the cool edge of the counter. "I spent the night with her."

"Okay, well, I forgive you for not texting me back." Amelia paused; there was a shuffling sound on the other end. "I'm getting comfortable…so…tell me everything."

The giddiness in Amelia's voice made River smile.

Clay popped the top on the last pale ale in her fridge and walked to where the unfinished canvas lay on the floor. She paced the edges of the work, slowly downing the icy beer. Thinking, feeling, aware of the elements around her. The cool concrete under her bare feet, the shafts of late afternoon light, particles illuminated in the air, the smell of honeysuckle, a bird call, and the brush of her loose-fitting jeans against tender skin. She'd put on a clean T-shirt and jeans after a shower, the rough denim a reminder of her glorious night with River. She'd been unable to shake the feel of River all day. Working seemed the only option, somewhere to put all she was feeling so she could return to it later, when River was gone.

She'd tried not to think about it, but it was impossible not to think about how River's presence here was brief, temporary. She'd likely be heading back to her life in the city in a few days. Would Clay have the courage to visit River in New York? She'd considered it, and she honestly didn't have an answer to that question. A week ago, she'd have said absolutely not. But after last night, maybe.

Clay finished the beer, cued up Sigur Ros in her playlist, and touched the album, *Valtari*. She slid the volume as high as it would go and closed her eyes as the haunting music reverberated off the hard surfaces around her. She stared at the array of liquid acrylic paints along the shelves for a few minutes, then returned to the canvas carrying yellow ochre, a deep gold, and a second jar of burnt sienna. She hovered above the canvas holding paint in each hand and then, as if conducting a symphony, drizzled the rich colors over the kinetic background from the night before.

To paint, in this moment, was to breathe.

Chapter Twenty-three

G litter Girl to Fast Break and Paintball, do you copy?" Grace's voice squawked over the radio in the tow truck.

"Paintball here, go ahead." Clay clicked off.

"Where are you?" Grace sounded stressed.

"On a pickup near the county line, about thirty minutes outside town. Are you okay?" She'd gotten a call late from AAA.

"This is Fast Break, I copy. What's up?" Trip cut in.

"Any chance you guys could meet me at Mosquito Alley for a powwow?"

Something must be up if Grace was calling a meeting on a Sunday night. Clay was itching to see River, but maybe a little break would help her gain some perspective, clear her head a little. And anyway, if Grace needed her, there was nothing more important.

"Paintball ETA about five thirty. I need to drop the truck off at the shop first." There'd be no room to park such a big vehicle roadside, plus she needed to offload the car she'd picked up. She'd ride the bike out to the river.

"Fast Break five thirty for me too. See you there."

"Thanks, guys. I'll bring food, and you bring drinks. Glitter Girl out."

"I'll be on the bike. Trip, can you throw in a beer or two for me? Over."

Thank goodness Grace was bringing food. A cooler didn't work so well on the Moto Guzzi.

"No problem. Fast Break out."

When she got to their special spot along the river, Trip's truck and Grace's battered Corolla were nowhere in sight. Clay followed the sandy path down to the water's edge and took her boots off.

It was quiet, except for the cicadas. It almost seemed as if they'd crescendo when the temperature climbed. That sound would always remind Clay of childhood summers. She took a deep breath and exhaled slowly, trying hard to match her body's rhythms to the water's slow, swirling passage. A dragonfly skittered across the surface, touching down in spots, causing rippled patterns on the surface.

Trip carried her flip-flops and towel in one hand and Playmate cooler in the other as she padded barefoot down the sandy path toward Clay. Nostalgic flashes of the three of them splashing in the river, drinking their first alcohol, and sharing secrets instantly peeled away adulthood. Trip must have sensed it too. She grinned broadly, dropped the cooler, and barreled down the path. Trip yelled a battle cry and flung her towel and shoes at Clay as she shot past. A thick, knotted rope dangled from a huge oak limb that stretched out over the water, and Trip launched from the small patch of sand to grab the rope and swung out as far as possible before dropping into the water.

Clay quickly stripped down to her boxers and undershirt and took a running leap. Trip came up sputtering just as Clay cannonballed into the water next to her. They laughed and splashed each other.

"So, what's up?"

"Not sure. Grace called this meeting." Clay paddled beside Trip until they were able to stand in chest deep water.

"Hey, where are you guys?"

"Speaking of Grace." Trip cupped her hands to yell back. "Cooling off. You're late."

"I could use a hand with the *food*," Grace called back.

"Did somebody mention food?" Clay hustled out of the water. Her shorts and tank top dripping, she grabbed Grace in a big wet hug. "Where's your swimsuit?"

Before Grace could answer, Trip hugged her from the back, soaking her from both sides.

"Who needs to swim when I have you guys?"

Clay helped Grace spread the picnic blanket, then sat at the corner of it, finger combing her hair back away from her face.

"Are you guys hungry? I brought all your favorites. Chicken wings, ribs, cracklings, and potato salad."

Trip cocked her head at Grace. "Now you're stalling. We know where the food is. What's up?"

Grace took a deep breath. "Dani Wingate."

"My Dani?" Trip sounded surprised at the news that Grace might be interested in her newest veterinarian.

"Well, she *is* Grace's type." Clay took a long swig of beer. She was happy that they were here to solve Grace's romantic problems. Clay wasn't quite ready to share the news that she and River had slept together. Her mind drifted and she made a point to refocus on Grace.

"And what exactly is my type?"

Clay exchanged glances with Trip.

"You know, like…us." Clay motioned with her thumb between herself and Trip.

"Handsome, butch, sporty…did I mention handsome?" Trip grinned.

"There's a significant difference between you guys and Dani." Grace sipped her wine, the food on her paper plate untouched.

"Should we be offended?" Clay looked at Trip teasingly, trying to lighten the mood.

"That's not what I mean." Grace scowled at Clay. "She doesn't even want to be around me."

"What makes you think that?" Trip asked.

"She barely speaks to me unless she has to, shies away if I get too close, tenses if I try to touch her, and goes to Savannah at least twice a week, probably to hook up."

Trip frowned. "You mean when I send her to the airport there to ship or pick up semen?"

"There goes my appetite." Clay dropped a half-eaten chicken wing to her napkin.

"This is breeding season and frozen semen is big business in the horse world."

"Too much information." Clay's weak stomach was on the brink of revolt.

Grace was lost in thought for a moment, staring out at the river. She flinched and shifted her focus when she realized they were both watching her. "What?"

"Are you—"

"No, no, no. I'm not falling for her. Really." Grace cut Clay off.

"Then why can't you look at us?" Trip asked.

"And why is your left eyebrow doing that little quirky arch it does when you're holding something back?" Clay leaned forward, with her elbows on her knees. "Did something happen after I saw you at the party?"

"No." Grace's response was a little too quick.

"Wait…What happened?" Trip was clearly annoyed that she'd missed out on this bit of news.

"Yesterday, at the cookout, Dani was dragging Grace down the hallway."

"It was nothing," Grace said.

"I'm not so sure." Clay gave Grace a sideways glance and reached for another chicken wing.

The color flushing Grace's cheeks gave her away.

"I'm not falling for her, and I probably won't. She doesn't seem interested. It's like she's afraid of connecting, I mean *really* connecting."

Clay wondered if Grace believed that, or was simply trying to convince herself. Grace had a tendency to sell herself short. She sometimes failed to realize how terrific she was. Now was the time to remind her.

"You know you're amazing, right?" Grace looked at Clay and smiled shyly.

"What do *you* want, Gracie?" Trip waited for a response as Grace searched the river for an answer.

"I don't know…I can't stop thinking about her." Grace turned toward them; her eyes glistened.

"I know what you mean." Clay wanted to take the words back the minute she'd uttered them.

"Wait, what?" Trip looked at her.

"Nothing."

"Come to think of it, why did you leave the cookout in such a hurry? You didn't even say good-bye. And you left River poolside looking kind of upset." Trip's attention was fully focused on Clay now.

"I don't want to talk about me. We're here for Grace, remember?"

"Too late," Grace chimed in.

"So? What happened?" Trip pressed her.

"We had a misunderstanding."

"And?" Her answer clearly hadn't satisfied Trip.

"We spent last night sorting it out." Clay's cheeks warmed under the scrutiny.

"All night?" The pitch of Grace's voice notched up.

"And this morning." Clay couldn't stop the smile, and she was sure she was blushing.

"I knew it." Grace was smiling now too, for a moment, the worry gone from her face. "I knew she was into you. That very first day under the maple tree, sitting on that stupid fake plastic deer."

"Yeah, well, it just took me a little longer to figure it out."

"Maybe you'll finally cheer up. I miss my pal, Clay." Trip reached over and playfully punched her shoulder.

"Okay, okay…enough about me. We're here to help Grace, remember?"

"Talking with you two always helps." Grace smiled. "More chicken? And don't forget the potato salad."

Clay and Trip reached for second helpings of both. Clay settled back, listening to Trip and Grace talk. They'd all been there for each other, in good times and bad. This was one of the things Clay missed in New York. Friends who loved you for who you truly were. Friends who knew your history well enough to push you when you needed to be pushed and were there to catch you when you faltered. Friendships such as this were to be cherished, never to be taken for granted.

Chapter Twenty-four

Clay was up early. She couldn't sleep. She stopped by to chat with Preston over an early coffee before heading to the shop. No one else was there when she arrived so she unlocked the door, opened the blinds, and started a pot of coffee for Eddie and her grandpa. She'd texted River to say good morning but hadn't gotten a reply yet. She'd thought of texting or calling River late last night, but that felt needy after keeping River in bed half the day Sunday. She dropped into a chair, newspaper in hand, skimming headlines while the coffee pot soothingly hummed nearby. She felt...happy. Yeah, that was it, happy. Almost too happy, and that made her nervous. When she was feeling elated some shit was no doubt about to go down.

She laughed to herself. She was the pessimistic ballast for River's optimism.

"What's funny?" her grandpa asked. He reached through the door for the broom.

"Certainly not the news." She smiled up at him. "Coffee's on. I'll bring you a cup when it's ready."

"Good. Some raccoon got into the trash can out back. I'm gonna go sweep that up." She nodded and he let the door slowly close behind him.

The day dragged on. River responded to Clay's text around ten o'clock. She was teasingly vague in the message. Obviously, she was going to make Clay work a little harder for that second date.

Around twelve thirty, Clay decided to make a quick run to her place to change. She'd worn the wrong shirt for the temperature. It'd been hard to tell how warm it was going to get when she'd left the house earlier, but she should have known better than to wear a long-sleeved shirt. The River fog was keeping her from thinking clearly.

She pushed through the door of her place, unfastened the first few buttons, and then pulled the shirt over her head and tossed it on the bed. There was a freestanding wardrobe in the far corner near the partial bathroom wall. Rummaging around for a minute or two finally produced a clean T-shirt. A trip to do laundry at her grandpa's house was becoming imperative.

Clay tugged the dark cotton shirt down. As her head popped through the neck of the shirt, she focused on what she'd missed when she first walked in.

The four remaining finished canvases, the ones she'd brought back with her from New York. They were gone. A glaring, vacant space along the wall stared back at her. Clay's stomach bottomed out. The first thought she had was that River had taken them.

This was the uneasy feeling she'd had earlier. That everything was too good to be true. She already knew there were people in the world you couldn't trust. That's why she'd come back to Pine Cone, leaving the cutthroat New York art scene behind.

Fuck.

She stood looking at the spot where the four paintings had been for several minutes, her temperature rising with each moment that passed.

Clay dug in her pocket for her phone and hit River's number.

❖

River's phone rang and she reached to grab it.

"Hello, River? It's Natalie Payne."

"Hi, Natalie."

"Listen, we got an offer on the house this morning."

River's phone buzzed. She had a second call. She held the screen up to see that it was from Clay. She'd much rather talk to Clay than Natalie but decided to let Clay's call go to voice mail. She'd call her back, or better yet, run by the shop and see Clay in person.

"River? Did I lose you?"

"No, I'm here, sorry. I just had a second call coming in."

"I'd like to bring the paperwork over later so that you can review the offer. What time works for you?"

River considered her schedule for the rest of the day. At the top of her agenda was Clay, so if she took care of things with Natalie sooner rather than later, then she'd be free for other things.

"You know, I'm at the house now if you want to bring them by anytime in the next hour or so. Would that work for you?"

"Perfect. I'll see you shortly."

River clicked off and was just about to check voice mail when her phone rang again. Her brother was finally calling her back. If he was in the mood to chat, she'd better take it. She'd left him two messages already, and it had taken until now for him to return her calls.

❖

River's voice mail picked up, and Clay silently contemplated leaving a message. But what she needed to say to River she should say in person. She was too angry right now anyway. She stormed out of the warehouse, revved the bike, and zoomed back to work. She was so pissed she almost ran a stop sign and had to check herself. Get her head out of her ass. She pulled to the curb, removed her helmet, and took several slow, deep breaths.

Would River be so ruthless as to take the paintings without asking? She couldn't quite picture it, and yet, who else would have done it? Who else?

Her phone buzzed in her pocket. It was River. She tried to slow her speeding heart as she answered the call.

"Clay?"

"Yeah." Fuck, she was pissed. Mostly at herself.

"Are you all right? You sound…different."

"Look, you got what you wanted, so let's just call it even."

"What? What are you talking about."

"Just go back to New York and leave me the fuck alone."

"Clay—"

She ended the call. She stared at the dark screen for a moment then switched her phone completely off and shoved it in her pocket. Whatever excuse River was going to give, she didn't want to hear it.

Back at the garage, she poured a cup of leftover morning coffee and didn't bother with milk to soften its bitterness. A faint line marked her lame rinse job from earlier, a stain halfway up the inside, like a watermark of bad choices. For all the times in her life she'd been wrong. Wrong about friends, wrong about lovers, just plain wrong.

Clay looked up as a squad car pulled toward the garage bay door. At first, she thought it was Grace but then realized it was

Jamie, Grace's new deputy. Eddie didn't seem to be around so she walked out to talk to Jamie.

"Can I help you with something?" She tried not to sound as angry as she felt, but she wasn't sure she succeeded. Jamie didn't really know her well enough to know the difference.

"Yeah, Grace said I should bring the car in for an oil change." Jamie stood in the open door of the car. "Say, do you mind if I let Petunia out for a minute?"

"No, there's nothing she can hurt around here, as long as she doesn't go toward the road." Clay reached down and patted the fluffy pooch.

"She's trained to stay close. Petunia, sit." Petunia sat on her fluffy haunches next to Clay's feet.

"Pull the car in and center it over that lift in the floor." Clay knelt beside Petunia sinking her fingers into her scruffy fur while Jamie positioned the car inside the garage.

Eddie could do the oil change as soon as he was back from delivering Mrs. Eldridge's car that now had four brand new tires, minus one road-weary tube sock. Of course, Bo could do the oil change, but sometime around lunch he'd slunk off and not returned. Clay ducked into the office to get the paperwork for Jamie to sign. She handed Jamie the clipboard at about the same moment Petunia barked from somewhere in the garage.

"Petunia only barks if she's found something." Jamie looked over her shoulder toward the corner of the garage.

"You mean, like a mouse?" Clay took the paperwork back from Jamie.

Jamie gave her an odd look. "No, usually something else."

Clay followed Jamie toward the sound of Petunia's barks. The dog was in the storage room. Clay switched on the light. Petunia was wagging her tail and barking at an old metal toolbox under a shelf in a darkened corner, half hidden behind a large metal bucket.

"Does this toolbox belong to you?"

"It's my grandfather's garage. All the tools, just about everything belongs to the business."

"Then I have your permission to open it?"

"Go ahead." Clay was curious to see what set the dog off.

Jamie used a flathead screwdriver from a nearby workbench to release the latch and open the lid, careful not to touch it. Once the lid was open, Petunia sat back and panted cheerfully. Clay leaned in for a closer look.

Inside the box were small clear bags of what looked like pills.

"What the hell? Those don't belong to Grandpa or me."

"Prescription drugs." Jamie poked around the toolbox, moving some of the bags aside to look underneath. "Looks like codeine, fentanyl, oxycodone, and probably hydrocodone."

"Fucking hell." Clay was already feeling pretty angry. Discovering someone was stashing drugs in her grandpa's garage was like throwing gasoline on a flame.

"Chances are someone started using these themselves and then started selling small quantities in order to keep their own supply up. All of these are highly addictive opioids."

"Well, they don't belong to me, or my grandpa, or Eddie… but I have a pretty good idea who put them there."

"Best not to assume anything until we dust this for prints." Jamie walked back toward the squad car and Clay followed her. "I'm going to call this in."

Jamie radioed Grace while Clay paced. This was the last thing she needed today. She'd made her pacing circuit only three times when Trip's double axel truck swung into a parking spot in front of the office. Trip gave Jamie a look as she walked toward Clay, but they didn't acknowledge each other. Still, it seemed like something was up. It didn't matter. Clay was too inside her own head at the moment to deal with anyone else's drama.

"What's going on?" Trip was still looking in Jamie's direction when she reached Clay's side.

"Petunia found a toolbox full of drugs in the storage room."

"No shit."

"Yeah, no shit." Clay crossed her arms and glared at the large, dark opening of the bay door. "Jamie is calling it in."

"Oh." Trip seemed nervous.

"What's up with you and Jamie?"

Trip gave her a funny look. "Nothing."

Whatever. If Trip didn't want to talk about it Clay wasn't in the mood to tease it out of her right now. She resumed her pacing.

"What's up with you? You're as tense as a long-tailed cat in a room full of rocking chairs." Trip was trying to joke, but Clay was not in the mood for humor.

"You mean besides finding a bunch of prescription drugs in the garage?" Clay wasn't ready to get into anything else with Trip. Especially with Grace likely to show up any minute.

Clay was about to say something else, but just then, Bo's truck appeared on the roadway. He slowed and turned in. He was still in the truck when Clay yelled at him.

"Hey, I need to talk to you." She took a few long strides toward him.

Recognition seemed to dawn on his stupid, scruffy face. His eyes darted toward Jamie as she got out of the squad car. He threw the truck in reverse, roared back, barely missing one of the gas pumps, and then spun gravel as his giant off-road tires bounced back up onto the paved road and took off.

"Asshole!" Clay looked back at Jamie. "I know those drugs belong to him."

"Who's him?" Jamie asked.

"Bo Mathis. He works here…barely."

"Listen, I can see you've got a lot going on here." Trip casually shifted her stance. "I just wanted to come by and tell you I picked up the paintings."

"What did you say?" Clay slowly turned. It was as if time screeched to a halt.

"I swung by your place this morning and picked up those four canvases. You told me a few weeks ago that I could hang them in the clinic."

"You…what?" Clay's brain was struggling to catch up.

"I swung by your place this morning and picked up those paintings. You told me a few months ago that I could hang them in the clinic. I tried to call, but I think your phone is off, or dead."

"I am such an asshole." Clay covered her face with her hands.

"I knew that already." Trip gave her shoulder a friendly punch. "But seriously, buddy, what is going on with you?"

"I'll explain, but first I need to make a quick call."

Chapter Twenty-five

River sank into the chair near her aunt's desk in the gallery. Clay was angry about something and she had no idea what. Surely she didn't mean what she'd said. After the night they'd spent together how could Clay talk to her that way?

After Clay hung up on her, she'd considered driving over to the garage and confronting her, but that would be the second time she'd chased after Clay. Not this time. Whatever was going on with Clay, River was going to wait for Clay to come to her. Maybe her initial assessment of Clay's status had been accurate. Maybe Clay wasn't emotionally available after all. Clearly, she wasn't getting past what had happened in New York. It was better that River knew the truth now, before she became more invested in where this might lead.

The paperwork Natalie had dropped off was on the desk in front of her. She scanned the offer again. Why had she hesitated to sign it? Didn't she want to be rid of this place? She could barely take care of the gallery in New York, much less a second gallery in Georgia.

River set the paper aside and scanned the space. She could see the whole place coming together if she stayed. She'd almost allowed herself to imagine it. Daydreams were swarming in her head when she heard the bell over the door chime. She must have forgotten to lock it after Natalie left. She couldn't see the door from where she was sitting in the gallery's small office.

The figure standing in the large, open front area was backlit by the windows.

"I'm sorry, we're not open right now."

"Not here to look at no art."

The man's voice sounded familiar. It wasn't until she was standing far too close that she realized the man was Bo Mathis.

"Hi, can I help you with something?" River tried for neutral, despite the fact that Bo's presence put her on edge.

"We're taking a drive. Get the keys to that truck and bring your phone."

"I don't know who you think you are, but I'm not going anywhere with you." She took a step back. "You need to leave now before I call the police."

"I saw the police already. Now, get them keys." He pulled a small revolver from behind his back and pointed at her.

River's heart rate spiked. She started to move away from him slowly, but he lunged for her, capturing her wrist.

"Let me go!" She tried to jerk away from his grasp, but instead he yanked her forward. He spoke close to her face.

"Tell me where the damn keys are."

"They're on the counter, in the kitchen." He smelled of cigarettes and sweat and bad ideas.

Bo dragged her through the house to the kitchen and wedged her body between his and the counter until she relented and reached for the keys with her free hand.

"Now, where's your phone?"

Instinctively, she looked toward the coffee table. He let go of her to pick up the phone, and she bolted for the door. But he was faster than he looked. He pinned her against the door, breathing, talking very close to her ear.

"You're a feisty one, I'll give you that." He wheeled her around. "Now, play nice and let's go for a drive. We'll call your girlfriend on the way."

This was about Clay. River's heart seized. Clay didn't care about her; why would Clay have anything to do with this?

"She's not my girlfriend."

"That's not the way it looked to me." He held her wrist tightly as he shoved her toward Clay's truck. He opened the passenger door. "Get in and then slide over. You're driving."

River reached down and slipped her shoe off.

"What are you doin'?"

"I can't drive in heels." She tossed first one and then the second shoe onto the seat with her free hand. It was broad daylight, but no one was around.

Bo jabbed the nose of the revolver into her ribs. "Get in, quit stalling."

Her mind raced. What were her options if he had a gun pointed at her?

"Why are you doing this? I don't even know you."

"Not everything is about you." He turned to look through the back window as she cranked the truck. "Back out and go that way." He pointed with the gun.

River did as she was told. It only took a few minutes for her to realize they were heading away from town, not toward it. Nausea washed over her, but she tamped it down. Keep it together. Think. Bo seemed nervous, on edge. He kept looking back as if he expected someone to be following them.

River's phone was on the seat between them, and when it rang, she jumped. Bo got to it first and answered it.

"Well now, I was just about to call you."

❖

Clay's heart rate spiked at the sound of Bo's voice. Wide-eyed, she spun to face Grace who was standing nearby talking to Jamie.

"What is it?" Grace took a step toward her.

"Bo, why are you answering River's phone?"

Grace froze.

"Cause me and your girl are taking a little drive." There was static or wind noise in the background. "Let's just say you've got something I need and I've got something you want."

"Bo, if you hurt one hair on her head I swear—"

Grace touched Clay's arm; she was shaking her head.

"I know you and that dog cop found my stuff. Bring it and you can have your girlfriend back."

"Where? Where are you?"

"Meet me at the old mill, just past the bridge." Bo paused. "And don't bring none of your lezzie friends, especially the cop."

"I won't. Just relax, Bo. I'll bring your shit. It's not like I want it here at the garage anyway. But you better not hurt River."

"She's pretty. Why would I want to hurt something so pretty?"

"Bo—"

He clicked off.

"Where is he?" Grace was all business, snapping into cop mode.

"He's got River. He wants me to bring his drugs and meet him at the mill in trade for River." Clay stomped around, dust flying up from her boot falls. "Damn it all to hell." She stopped and looked at Grace. "I'm going."

"No, you're not." Grace was firm.

"He said for me to come by myself. He specifically told me not to bring you. So, I'm going." She squared off in front of Grace.

"No, you're not. You're gonna stay here with Jamie who's gonna call this in. She looked at Jamie. "Tell them we have a hostage situation underway and that drugs are involved. Who knows if Bo is under the influence of something himself."

"It would explain a lot." Clay swept her fingers through her hair. "God, I'm such an idiot."

Trip rested her hand on Clay's shoulder. It was small comfort. All Clay could think about was getting River back. And then beating Bo to a pulp with her bare hands. Grace started to get into her squad car.

"He'll see you and he'll do something stupid. He said no cops."

"Clay, I've got this." Grace's voice was steady, even. "He's not going to hurt River. He'll take the Mill Road, that's the fastest route and the most secluded. Trust me, he'll never see me coming. I'll approach on foot. Now, let me do my job."

"Aren't you going to wait for backup or something? Isn't that how this works?"

"I think I can handle one redneck." Grace closed the door and backed the car away from where Clay was standing. Dust swirled in little sideways tornados as she whipped the cruiser onto the paved road and sped off.

For a second, Clay just stood there, then she turned and looked at Trip.

"What?"

"Give me your keys." Clay held out her hand to Trip.

"No way. You can't just go charging in there." Trip shook her head and backed away from Clay.

"Give me your damn keys. I'm not gonna let Grace go in there by herself, and I'm not taking any chances of losing River, not now, not ever." Her outstretched hand hovered in the air between them, and Trip just stared at her for what seemed like forever, but in reality, was probably only seconds.

"I'm driving." Trip turned and strode toward her truck. "You're all wound up and in no condition to drive."

Clay followed her, with Jamie shouting after them.

"Hey, where are you going?" She half stood in the door of the squad car, the radio mic in her hand, and Petunia sitting nearby, panting, with a smile on her shaggy face. But it was too late to respond.

Trip followed Grace's exit along the paved road. When they reached the Mill Road, she took a hard right. A huge dust storm followed the double axel truck down the unpaved dirt road. They could see a faint trail of dust about a quarter mile ahead. She figured that was Grace.

Clay clenched and unclenched her fist, pounded against her thigh. All the things she wished she'd said to River looped endlessly through her head. She'd jumped to conclusions about River and she hated that about herself. River had been nothing but honest with her, and kind, and encouraging. The first misunderstanding between them and Clay had thrown all of it under the bus and let her temper, insecurities, and the emotional baggage she'd carried with her from New York ruin everything. So stupid. So, so stupid.

River glanced sideways at Bo. He kept checking the side mirror as if he was afraid someone would follow them. Then River saw something in the rearview mirror and a tendril of hope rose in her chest. The faintest hint of a dust cloud somewhere past the curve in the road behind them. Just a hint of it was visible above the trees past the curve. She needed to distract Bo before he saw it too. The revelation that she was not in this alone, that someone was coming, rallied her courage.

The road was becoming rough and rutted as it neared the river. They passed the bridge where she'd danced with Clay. The memory was like a punch in the stomach now. After the way Clay had talked to her over the phone earlier. Her heart beat like a drum; she was pissed.

"Slow down!"

In her anger, she'd obviously accelerated without realizing it. This was the perfect distraction.

"If you wanted to drive like a grandma then you shouldn't have put me behind the wheel." She swerved as a particularly deep groove in the road caught the front tire.

Bo bounced against the doorframe. It registered for the first time that he wasn't wearing his seat belt.

"I said fucking slow down!"

"Or what?" River white knuckled the steering wheel with both hands and glared at him. "I didn't ask for this…I didn't ask for any of this."

Her shoes bumped her leg as they bounced on the seat between them. She grabbed for one and threw it at Bo. The shoe ricocheted off his temple. The surprised look on his face told her he hadn't expected her to put up much of a fight. This realization only served to fan the flame. Rage surged in her chest as she righted the truck on the rough dirt.

River was no Atomic Blonde, but she certainly wasn't above pummeling a guy with a high-heeled shoe. She grabbed the remaining shoe and swung it repeatedly at his face. She did her best to get his left eye with the heel of it. Bo raised his arm to deflect her frenzied assault, but the truck was bouncing so hard he needed to hang on with one arm, since he still had the gun in the other.

The truck was going too fast now, and River fought to keep it on the road with one hand. She flung the shoe at Bo and yanked the wheel with both hands, but it was too late. The truck lurched off the road and bounced hard over a particularly deep rut. Bo's elbow hit the metal doorframe hard and the gun discharged, shattering the windshield in front of River. She screamed and covered her face as the old pickup flung itself over the shoulder, down the embankment, and into the Altamaha River.

Without the restraint of the seat belt, Bo's head bounced against the dashboard like one of those crash dummies they use to test airbags. The truck hit hard and then there was a whooshing sound as the truck slowly sank below the surface. Water filled the floorboard and now was pouring in through the windows and the shattered windshield. River wrestled with the seat belt. Water was up to her chest when it finally released, and she pulled herself through the window and stroked backward away from the truck.

She was treading water, waiting to see if Bo followed, but he didn't. A squad car came to an abrupt stop near where the truck had gone off the road and Grace got out.

"Swim this way, River. Over to me." Grace unclipped her utility belt and dropped it to the ground.

The top of the truck was almost completely under water and disappearing quickly. River glanced back and forth between the sinking truck and Grace.

"What are you doing? River, no."

She heard Grace call to her right before she dropped under the water's surface. She swam back to the truck. He was unconscious and his head lolled just above the rising water. River couldn't save herself and watch Bo drown, even if he was an asshole. Sure, he'd fired the gun at her, but she was pretty sure it was accidental.

River swam to the other side of the cab and tugged at the door. It wouldn't open. She climbed onto the sunken hood of the truck and reached through the missing windshield for the collar of his shirt. The truck was sinking fast now. With both feet braced on the frame around where the windshield had been, she heaved with all her might. As his upper body cleared the frame, she grabbed him under his arms and tugged. The rising water eased his body weight, and with a bit more effort, she pulled him free. She dragged him by the collar like an empty canoe up onto shore, leaving his legs to sink under the water's edge. Then she scrambled up the bank for fear he'd come to and she'd be right back where she started.

"Are you all right?" Grace asked.

"I'm okay..." Her breath came in gasps. "But I need...to get away...from him. He's all yours." River swept her hands through her wet hair and started walking barefoot back the way they'd come.

At the edge of the road, she turned to see the cab of Clay's truck sink farther, now barely visible beneath the water's surface.

Chapter Twenty-six

Clay leaned forward in an attempt to see past the dust. Grace must be just ahead of them. She saw something, someone, in the road.

"Stop! Stop the truck!" Clay opened the door while the vehicle was still in motion.

"Clay, wait." Trip called after her, but she was out the door as soon as Trip hit the brakes.

And then Clay saw her, a hazy figure through the dust. River was walking barefoot down the road. Clay ran toward her. She swept River up in her arms, lifting her feet off the ground.

"River, thank God you're okay." Clay set her down, held her face between her hands, and checked for injury. "I'm so sorry…I'm so sorry about everything."

River leaned into her and Clay cradled her head against her chest. Her wet hair soaked into Clay's shirt.

"Are you hurt?"

River shook her head. Tears were welling up in her eyes.

"Where is Bo?" She wanted badly to take a few swings at him with a tire iron.

"He's up there, just past that clump of trees." River pointed, and her voice broke. "We went off the road, and I left him on the embankment near your truck. Grace is with him."

Trip was there now. She draped a blanket from her truck around River's shoulders. It wasn't cold, but she was shivering, either from fear, or shock, or something else. Clay tugged the blanket tightly around her and drew her close, kissing her forehead and stroking her back.

"I was such a jerk on the phone today. Please forgive me."

"Yeah, what was that about?" River's voice was muffled against her chest.

"Just my stupid insecure ego. It wasn't anything you did; it was all me."

They were quiet for a minute, and Clay relished the feel of River in her arms.

"I'm sorry about your truck." River tipped her head up a little to look at Clay.

"Who cares about an old truck?"

"You probably did."

Clay laughed. She tightened her embrace, snuggling River closer.

"You had to crash to find me, and then you had to crash again so I could find you." Clay kissed her hair lightly. "You're driving is terrible, but your aim is true."

River's hand was at the back of Clay's head now. Her eyes lured Clay in until their lips touched, lightly at first and then with intensity. Clay angled her head, taking River in, possessively deepening the kiss.

When they came up for breath, Clay tightened her arms around River. "I was so scared."

River looked up. "Me too."

"You're safe now." Clay rubbed River's back through the blanket.

River tucked her head under Clay's chin.

When Clay looked down, she realized River was barefoot. And despite the terrible circumstances that led to this moment, she couldn't help smiling.

"Where are your shoes?"

"Oh." She looked down too as if she'd forgotten until just now that she had them. "Halfway to Savannah by now, I guess."

Clay squeezed her shoulders. "What'd I tell you? A country girl in a city girl's body."

River's eyes glistened. "Well, this city girl has two requests."

"Name them."

"Take my hand...and take me home."

Clay entwined their fingers. Her heart felt light as she and River walked hand in hand toward Trip's truck.

The plan was to drop River off on the way to Trip's to borrow a vehicle, but River was feeling a bit shaken and didn't want to be alone. Clay reached across the console of Trip's fire engine red Jeep Wrangler and clasped River's hand. She'd insisted they stop by the diner and pick up takeout because she suspected River still didn't have much more than cheese and crackers at her aunt's place.

She parked in the driveway and walked around to open the door for River, who still seemed a bit dazed. Clay took the bag of food off her lap and held her hand again as River hopped down.

"The first thing I want to do is take a shower."

"Go ahead, this fried chicken will keep." Clay followed River inside and put the food on the counter.

River walked slowly down the hallway toward the bathroom as if she were sleepwalking. River left the door ajar so that Clay could hear the water running. She paced around the kitchen for a couple of minutes until she could stand it no longer. She ripped off her T-shirt as she walked down the hall, leaving her jeans and shoes at the door.

River swept her hands over her hair as the hot water pelted her face. Her hands were shaking, and she placed them flat on the tile in front of her to steady them. She wasn't sure how long she'd been standing like that when she felt Clay's arms encircle her waist. Clay kissed her shoulder and pressed against her back. She sighed and allowed Clay to hold her.

"You're okay, you're safe," Clay whispered.

She rotated in Clay's arms. "I am now."

She tilted her head up until their lips met. They kissed languidly, unhurriedly, as if time was theirs to use as they pleased.

Clay lathered River's skin with soap. Then shampooed her hair. River allowed Clay to attend to her. Clay's strong, sure hands moving across her slick skin soothed her, grounded her.

In the midst of the harrowing ride with Bo, she'd at first been scared, then angry, and then scared again when the gun discharged. Seeing Clay running toward her after losing the truck in the river made her realize how much she wanted Clay. Not just today, but tomorrow, and possibly forever. She leaned into Clay now as Clay wrapped a towel around her shoulders and used a second towel to dry her hair.

"Clay, I need to talk to you." Her voice broke.

Clay held River's face in her hands and kissed her forehead.

"Let's get you some clothes first."

"No."

Clay arched her eyebrows.

"For what I have to say, I don't want any barriers between us." She tugged Clay, still naked, toward the bedroom.

Under the light covering, River snuggled into Clay's shoulder, her still-damp hair fanned out across the pillow. She lay on her side, facing Clay. She traced the outline of Clay's jaw with her fingertip.

"River, I—"

"Me first." She covered Clay's lips with her fingers. "I know that you've been really hurt and that trust for you is difficult. Trust is a fragile thing. Once truly broken it's almost impossible to repair. I know that. And I do not take the responsibility of someone's trust lightly." She paused. "I want you to know you can trust me."

"I know."

"Clay, I'm…I'm in love with you." River cut her off when Clay opened her mouth to reply. "I think I knew that the first time I saw you climb off that motorcycle and walk toward the door." She stroked Clay's face tenderly with her hand. "I know we haven't known each other very long, but sometimes… sometimes I think you just know."

Clay smiled. "Fools rush in."

"What?"

"The night we danced in the moonlight and you asked me if I thought it was true, that fools rush in." Clay rolled on top of River, with her thigh between River's legs. "I don't feel foolish, but I've definitely fallen hard for you. Holding you in my arms that night, even before we kissed…I think that's when I knew."

"So you feel it too?" Relief surged through River's system.

Clay brushed loose strands of hair away from her face. "I feel it." Clay moved her hand down and began to caress River's breast. Her lips lightly brushed River's. "Is this okay?" Clay whispered.

"Yes." River draped her arms around Clay's neck and arched into Clay. "Yes, most definitely yes."

Clay watched the last rays of evening light fall across River's face, dancing in her eyes. Things felt different between them now. Clay realized she wasn't afraid any more. She *did* trust River. Kissing, caressing, exploring, possessively laying claim to River's body. Whenever she shifted, River filled the spaces, creating something whole. River had been what was missing.

She raised up so that she could see River's face as she climaxed. Head back, eyes closed, her mouth forming soundless words. When at last River relaxed in her arms, River's head fell back to the pillow, and Clay feathered soft kisses across her cheek, down her neck, returning to her lips.

"River…"

"Yes?" River's voice was soft, breathless.

The simplest words sometimes had the most power.

"I love you."

Clay had taken a tremendous running leap, to rush in, to risk everything for a boundless love. River's lashes fluttered and then she met Clay's waiting gaze. She smiled.

"I love you, too."

"Stay with me."

"For how long?" River caressed Clay's face.

"Forever."

"Forever might not be long enough." River drew Clay down until their lips met.

Clay sank into River. Nothing separated them now, and together they were creating something new. The dark places, the what-ifs, no longer haunted Clay. With River in her arms, Clay was only thinking of what was possible. And at the moment, the possibilities seemed limitless. Boundless.

Epilogue

Clay watched River scrunch her cute nose from across the small table. A bud vase with two daisies separated them. The light from the window bounced like little starbursts off her water glass.

"Not good?"

River chewed slowly.

"They're okay. I'm ruined now. I will settle for no less than the real thing." River had suggested they eat lunch at the Whistle Stop Café near her apartment in Chelsea. "I'm thinking fried green tomatoes taste much better in Georgia. It must be the humidity."

"Or our Southern affinity for salt and cornmeal."

River laughed. "Maybe."

"Trying to make something healthy and fried at the same time just never works. You've gotta go all in, throw caloric caution to the wind." Clay reached across with her fork to sample from River's plate. She chewed slowly as if she were some sort of culinary connoisseur. "Nope, not enough batter and definitely not enough salt."

"Also, out of season."

"Yes, not the same at all as vine-ripe tomatoes."

It had been six months since River had driven Clay's old Ford into the Altamaha. Bodean Mathis had been convicted of kidnapping, carrying an unlicensed firearm, and possession of a controlled substance with the intent to sell. He was currently cooling his heels at a maximum-security facility for men in west Texas. Bo's mother had taken the whole scandalous affair pretty hard, but Clay's grandpa was doing his best to distract her with evening strolls and long talks on her porch swing. Mrs. Mathis was a nice woman. Clay didn't fault her for Bo's shortcomings. Drugs could do things to people. Turn them into someone you never thought they'd be. Bo was never the sort of upstanding young man his mother had dreamed he'd be, and the drugs just made all of it worse.

"Are we having dessert?" River's voice called Clay back to the moment. "I was thinking you might like to sample the key lime pie."

"Clay?"

Veronica, resplendent in a deep blue silk Bottega Veneta dress, had materialized out of nowhere. Or maybe every other woman simply ceased to exist for Clay when River was around.

"Hello, Veronica." Clay dabbed at her lips with her napkin.

"I didn't know you were back in New York." Veronica glanced from Clay to River.

"Veronica, this is River Hemsworth. River, this is Veronica." River knew who Veronica was, but she wanted to be sure Veronica acknowledged River.

"Hello." River extended her hand and Veronica took it.

"You own the Hemsworth Gallery, right?"

"I used to."

"You sold it?" Veronica seemed surprised.

"To my partner, Amelia Glass."

Clay could tell Veronica was dying to ask more, but didn't. Instead she switched her attention back to Clay. She even rotated her stance, dismissing River's presence.

"Maybe we could get together some night this week. It's been too long, and it would be great to catch up." Veronica lightly touched Clay's shoulder for emphasis.

"Thanks for the offer, but I'm busy."

"All week?"

"Pretty much forever."

Veronica's lips parted as if she was about to say something, but then she didn't. She glanced back at River and then turned to Clay, who simply smiled.

"I see." Veronica quirked a sculpted eyebrow and nodded. "Well, it was a pleasure seeing you. I wish you the best."

With that, Veronica sashayed to the door in her untenable heels and was gone.

"Was she wishing me the best, or you?" River took a sip of her water and then smiled.

"Regardless of who she was talking to, I'm pretty sure she didn't mean it."

River laughed.

"Let's get out of here." Clay tugged her jacket on and fished her wallet out of her back pocket. She left more than enough cash on the table to cover the bill plus tip, stood up, and extended her hand for River to take it.

They strolled along the busy street for three blocks before the small, understated sign for the Hemsworth Gallery came into view. Amelia had decided to keep the name for now, even though she'd bought River's interest in the business entirely. This was Amelia's gallery now. Clay stopped in front of it. Seeing her name painted in bold san serif type across the front window of the gallery sent butterflies into a frenzy in her stomach. No matter how many gallery shows she did, Clay figured the nerves would always be there.

Purely representational art was not always truth. Everything she thought, everything she felt, was on those abstract canvases hanging along the walls inside. And tonight, everyone would be there, milling around, commenting on things that mattered most, maybe only to her.

"Are you regretting that we're not staying for the opening?"

Clay shook her head. They'd stayed in New York long enough to take care of things for River, and to hang the show, but they had an afternoon flight back to Atlanta, then a long drive to Pine Cone.

"Are you regretting that you sold the gallery?" Clay looked at River.

"No." They were standing side by side in front of the huge plate glass window. River looped her arm through Clay's and rested her cheek on Clay's shoulder. "I have this really sweet gallery in this charming town called Pine Cone that I can't wait to get back to."

Clay could feel herself smiling, all the way to her toes. She leaned in and kissed the top of River's head.

"Let's go home, my love."

They strolled arm in arm past trendy storefronts and coffee shops. As they passed a small park, dry leaves swirled around their feet, the last remnants of autumn in its transition to winter. They wound their way through pedestrian traffic and street noise toward River's apartment, where the last box had been packed two hours ago and loaded on a truck bound for Georgia.

The End

About the Author

Missouri Vaun spent a large part of her childhood in southern Mississippi, before attending high school in North Carolina and college in Tennessee. Strong connections to her roots in the rural South have been a grounding force throughout her life. Vaun spent twelve years finding her voice working as a journalist in places as disparate as Chicago, Atlanta, and Jackson, MS, all along filing away characters and their stories. Her novels are heartfelt, earthy, and speak of loyalty and our responsibility to others. She and her wife currently live in northern California.

Books Available from Bold Strokes Books

Alias by Cari Hunter. A car crash leaves a woman with no memory and no identity. Together with Detective Bronwen Pryce, she fights to uncover a truth that might just kill them both. (978-1-63555-221-8)

Death in Time by Robyn Nyx. Working in the past is hell on your future. (978-1-63555-053-5)

Hers to Protect by Nicole Disney. High school sweethearts Kaia and Adrienne will have to see past their differences and survive the vengeance of a brutal gang if they want to be together. (978-1-63555-229-4)

Of Echoes Born by 'Nathan Burgoine. A collection of queer fantasy short stories set in Canada from Lambda Literary Award finalist 'Nathan Burgoine. (978-1-63555-096-2)

Perfect Little Worlds by Clifford Mae Henderson. Lucy can't hold the secret any longer. Twenty-six years ago, her sister did the unthinkable. (978-1-63555-164-8)

Room Service by Fiona Riley. Interior designer Olivia likes stability, but when work brings footloose Savannah into her world and into a new city every month, Olivia must decide if what makes her comfortable is what makes her happy. (978-1-63555-120-4)

Sparks Like Ours by Melissa Brayden. Professional surfers Gia Malone and Elle Britton can't deny their chemistry on and off the beach. But only one can win... (978-1-63555-016-0)

Take My Hand by Missouri Vaun. River Hemsworth arrives in Georgia intent on escaping quickly, but when she crashes her Mercedes into the Clip 'n Curl, sexy Clay Cahill ends up rescuing more than her car. (978-1-63555-104-4)

The Last Time I Saw Her by Kathleen Knowles. Lane Hudson only has twelve days to win back Alison's heart. That is if she can gather the courage to try. (978-1-63555-067-2)

Wayworn Lovers by Gun Brooke. Will agoraphobic composer Giselle Bonnaire and Tierney Edwards, a wandering soul who can't remain in one place for long, trust in the passionate love destiny hands them? (978-1-62639-995-2)

Breakthrough by Kris Bryant. Falling for a sexy ranger is one thing, but is the possibility of love worth giving up the career Kennedy Wells has always dreamed of? (978-1-63555-179-2)

Certain Requirements by Elinor Zimmerman. Phoenix has always kept her love of kinky submission strictly behind the bedroom door and inside the bounds of romantic relationships, until she meets Kris Andersen. (978-1-63555-195-2)

Dark Euphoria by Ronica Black. When a high-profile case drops in Detective Maria Diaz's lap, she forges ahead only to discover this case, and her main suspect, aren't like any other. (978-1-63555-141-9)

Fore Play by Julie Cannon. Executive Leigh Marshall falls hard for Peyton Broader, her golf pro…and an ex-con. Will she risk sabotaging her career for love? (978-1-63555-102-0)

Love Came Calling by CA Popovich. Can a romantic looking for a long-term, committed relationship and a jaded cynic too busy for love conquer life's struggles and find their way to what matters most? (978-1-63555-205-8)

Outside the Law by Carsen Taite. Former sweethearts Tanner Cohen and Sydney Braswell must work together on a federal task force to see justice served, but will they choose to embrace their second chance at love? (978-1-63555-039-9)

The Princess Deception by Nell Stark. When journalist Missy Duke realizes Prince Sebastian is really his twin sister Viola in disguise, she plays along, but when sparks flare between them, will the double deception doom their fairy-tale romance? (978-1-62639-979-2)

The Smell of Rain by Cameron MacElvee. Reyha Arslan, a wise and elegant woman with a tragic past, shows Chrys that there's still beauty to embrace and reason to hope despite the world's cruelty. (978-1-63555-166-2)

The Talebearer by Sheri Lewis Wohl. Liz's visions show her the faces of the lost and the killers who took their lives. As one by one, the murdered are found, a stranger works to stop Liz before the serial killer is brought to justice. (978-1-635550-126-6)

White Wings Weeping by Lesley Davis. The world is full of discord and hatred, but how much of it is just human nature when an evil with sinister intent is invading people's hearts? (978-1-63555-191-4)

A Call Away by KC Richardson. Can a businesswoman from a big city find the answers she's looking for, and possibly love, on a small-town farm? (978-1-63555-025-2)

Berlin Hungers by Justine Saracen. Can the love between an RAF woman and the wife of a Luftwaffe pilot, former enemies, survive in besieged Berlin during the aftermath of World War II? (978-1-63555-116-7)

Blend by Georgia Beers. Lindsay and Piper are like night and day. Working together won't be easy, but not falling in love might prove the hardest job of all. (978-1-63555-189-1)

Hunger for You by Jenny Frame. Principe of an ancient vampire clan Byron Debrek must save her one true love from falling into the hands of her enemies and into the middle of a vampire war. (978-1-63555-168-6)

Mercy by Michelle Larkin. FBI Special Agent Mercy Parker and psychic ex-profiler Piper Vasey learn to love again as they race to stop a man with supernatural gifts who's bent on annihilating humankind. (978-1-63555-202-7)

Pride and Porters by Charlotte Greene. Will pride and prejudice prevent these modern-day lovers from living happily ever after? (978-1-63555-158-7)

Rocks and Stars by Sam Ledel. Kyle's struggle to own who she is and what she really wants may end up landing her on the bench and without the woman of her dreams. (978-1-63555-156-3)

The Boss of Her: Office Romance Novellas by Julie Cannon, Aurora Rey, and M. Ullrich. Going to work never felt so good. Three office romance novellas from talented writers Julie Cannon, Aurora Rey, and M. Ullrich. (978-1-63555-145-7)

The Deep End by Ellie Hart. When family ties become entangled in murder and deception, it's time to find a way out… (978-1-63555-288-1)

A Country Girl's Heart by Dena Blake. When Kat Jackson gets a second chance at love, following her heart will prove the hardest decision of all. (978-1-63555-134-1)

Dangerous Waters by Radclyffe. Life, death, and war on the home front. Two women join forces against a powerful opponent, nature itself. (978-1-63555-233-1)

Fury's Death by Brey Willows. When all we hold sacred fails, who will be there to save us? (978-1-63555-063-4)

It's Not a Date by Heather Blackmore. Kade's desire to keep things with Jen on a professional level is in Jen's best interest. Yet what's in Kade's best interest…is Jen. (978-1-63555-149-5)

Killer Winter by Kay Bigelow. Just when she thought things could get no worse, homicide Lieutenant Leah Samuels learns the woman she loves has betrayed her in devastating ways. (978-1-63555-177-8)

Score by MJ Williamz. Will an addiction to pain pills destroy Ronda's chance with the woman she loves or will she come out on top and score a happily ever after? (978-1-62639-807-8)

Spring's Wake by Aurora Rey. When wanderer Willa Lange falls for Provincetown B&B owner Nora Calhoun, will past hurts and a fifteen-year age gap keep them from finding love? (978-1-63555-035-1)

The Northwoods by Jane Hoppen. When Evelyn Bauer, disguised as her dead husband, George, travels to a Northwoods logging camp to work, she and the camp cook Sarah Bell forge a friendship fraught with both tenderness and turmoil. (978-1-63555-143-3)

Truth or Dare by C. Spencer. For a group of six lesbian friends, life changes course after one long snow-filled weekend. (978-1-63555-148-8)

A Heart to Call Home by Jeannie Levig. When Jessie Weldon returns to her hometown after thirty years, can she and her childhood crush Dakota Scott heal the tragic past that links them? (978-1-63555-059-7)

Children of the Healer by Barbara Ann Wright. Life becomes desperate for ex-soldier Cordelia Ross when the indigenous aliens of her planet are drawn into a civil war and old enemies linger in the shadows. Book Three of the Godfall Series. (978-1-63555-031-3)

Hearts Like Hers by Melissa Brayden. Coffee shop owner Autumn Primm is ready to cut loose and live a little, but is the baggage that comes with out-of-towner Kate Carpenter too heavy for anything long term? (978-1-63555-014-6)

Love at Cooper's Creek by Missouri Vaun. Shaw Daily flees corporate life to find solace in the rural Blue Ridge Mountains, but escapism eludes her when her attentions are captured by small town beauty Kate Elkins. (978-1-62639-960-0)

Somewhere Over Lorain Road by Bud Gundy. Over forty years after murder allegations shattered the Esker family, can Don Esker find the true killer and clear his dying father's name? (978-1-63555-124-2)

Twice in a Lifetime by PJ Trebelhorn. Detective Callie Burke can't deny the growing attraction to her late friend's widow, Taylor Fletcher, who also happens to own the bar where Callie's sister works. (978-1-63555-033-7)

Undiscovered Affinity by Jane Hardee. Will a no strings attached affair be enough to break Olivia's control and convince Cardic that love does exist? (978-1-63555-061-0)

BOLDSTROKESBOOKS.COM

Looking for your next great read?

Visit BOLDSTROKESBOOKS.COM
to browse our entire catalog of paperbacks, ebooks,
and audiobooks.

Want the first word on what's new?
Visit our website for event info,
author interviews, and blogs.

Subscribe to our free newsletter for sneak peeks,
new releases, plus first notice of promos
and daily bargains.

SIGN UP AT
BOLDSTROKESBOOKS.COM/signup

Bold Strokes Books
Quality and Diversity in LGBTQ Literature

*Bold Strokes Books is an award-winning publisher
committed to quality and diversity in LGBTQ fiction.*